The Lake George Casino Gamble

Book 2 of the Lake George Mystery and Adventure Series

By David Cederstrom

Second Edition

ISBN 978-0-9849403-5-6

A North Country Photographers production
Cover design and all photographs by David Cederstrom
Cover photo: Lake George

Prologue/Flash Forward

The latest affront by Sheriff's Department Investigator Alan McMendell ran hot through Carl Grisham's mind as Grisham stalked through the second floor of his imposing stone mansion on the west shore of Lake George.

Grisham recalled how McMendell had been an irritant ever since they were high school classmates 20-some years earlier. It had only grown worse when the big, dumb jock became a big, dumb cop.

Just a minute earlier, McMendell really pushed the envelope. Entering Grisham's home, making accusations, when Grisham had a party going on, for Chrissake. Then the big S.O.B. had the nerve to leave before Grisham had a chance to yell at him properly.

Grisham grimaced as a muffled burst of laughter drifted up from the cocktail party still going strong down on the first floor.

He entered his second-floor office and headed for the solace of his massive oak desk, sized to match the acreage of the room.

His blood pressure spiked even higher at the sight of documents scattered across the desk. He made a mental note to rake his secretary over the coals for this infraction when she came back to work the next morning.

Grisham felt a tap on his shoulder.

He spun around, his heart abruptly pounding from more than just anger. He hadn't heard a sound.

He relaxed when he saw who stood there.

"What the hell do you..." Grisham began.

He gasped as the knife slammed into his chest.

The point of the blade skittered painfully down his ribs, then plunged deep into his belly just under the ribcage.

Grisham froze, mind and body.

Then he saw the look of satisfaction in his attacker's eyes.

Grisham's mind scrambled to back into gear, fueled by a fresh surge of anger. Let *this* son of a bitch kill him? No way.

Grisham lashed out with a foot. It connected. Hard.

Probably a shin, Grisham thought. *Too bad. A knee would've been better.*

Still, Grisham was rewarded with a sharp hiss of pain from his attacker.

The driving pressure on the knife slackened momentarily.

Grisham pushed himself off that terrible blade and rolled backwards over the top of his desk.

Pain lanced through his torso. Worse than when the knife went in.

Grisham ignored it.

He felt the world slowing down around him. Adrenaline rush. He knew he was actually moving at lightning speed.

Which was good. He also knew he didn't have much time. He sensed the malignant presence of his attacker looming over him.

Grisham reached up under his desk for the classic M1911A1 Colt .45 automatic mounted there.

Locked and loaded, with a round in the chamber.

Grisham pulled the gun out of its mount with the smooth motion he had practiced many times. His thumb swiped off the safety almost instantly.

"Try to kill me, you bastard?" he tried to shout, but the words came out oddly hoarse.

Then his finger was on the trigger and squeezing.

Grisham felt the recoil pounding his hand, but barely noticed the blast of the three gunshots.

The presence looming over him disappeared.

Then Grisham was on his feet. No idea how he got there from the floor.

Mr. Thought-He-Could-Kill-Me-With-A-Knife wasn't down. Running for the door.

Grisham squeezed off three more rounds. A bullet splintered the door jamb a hundredth of a second after the bastard disappeared into the hall.

Grisham took a step to pursue. He reconsidered when the room started to spin.

"Dammit," he snarled, but he knew better than to keep going.

Grisham sat heavily in his black leather swivel chair. *Dammit again.*

His favorite chair, getting all bloody.

The world around him began ratcheting back up to normal speed.

The Colt was getting heavy. Grisham set it down on the desk.

He thought about the phone.

911.

Ambulance.

His arms were getting really heavy now, though.

Then he remembered McMendell. Yeah, the big fucking cop was still right outside in the yard. Heard the shots, no doubt. A frigging house full of party guests, but Grisham knew McMendell would be the one to call the ambulance. Probably render first aid, too, before the EMTs arrived.

Dammit three times.

McMendell, of all the damned people, was going to save his life.

Grisham sighed.

He felt his eyes closing.

Well, survival was survival. That's what mattered.

"Wake up, Grisham."

The vicious tone in the voice startled Grisham. Not what you'd expect from an EMT, or even McMendell.

Grisham opened his eyes.

He saw a gun aimed at his forehead. Small caliber.

Maybe a .22.

He saw the face behind it.

Dammit!

"You?" Grisham said.

The face nodded.

Sheriff's Department Investigator Alan McMendell leaned his 220 pounds of muscle and bone against his old Ford Taurus, parked on Carl Grisham's lawn along with a couple dozen other vehicles whose owners were inside enjoying Grisham's party.

Alan breathed in the night air, heavy with wet shoreline smells from the lake mixed with the fading bouquet of a lawn that must have been freshly mowed that afternoon.

He struggled to wrestle his agitation under control.

Sure, Grisham had the legal right to kick Alan out of his house, but Alan didn't have to like it.

Especially with a gunshot deputy in the hospital, and Grisham a potential suspect. Or, at the very least, likely to know something about it. Like maybe the shooter was Grisham's lowlife son, Kenny.

Alan took a few more deep breaths.

When his pulse slowed back to near normal, he flipped open his cellphone to call the DA to start the process of obtaining a warrant.

Three loud *bangs* stopped him.

Gunshots? In the house, maybe upstairs? Sounded like.

Three more bangs.

Gunshots! Definitely. Heavy caliber.

Drawing his Glock .40 S&W, Alan reached Grisham's front door in seconds and wrenched it open.

He was halfway to the stairs, using his imposing size to shove his way through the confused party crowd, when a seventh shot sounded.

A lighter caliber this time.

Maybe a .22.

Warren Street, Glens Falls, before dawn.

Chapter 1.

Four days earlier.

Holding his department-issue Glock .40 S&W in sweaty hands, Alan McMendell peered uneasily into the dim, pre-dawn twilight in the quiet Glens Falls neighborhood, seeking any sign of Kenny Grisham, the heavily-armed young man he was hunting.

Alan's wary, restless brown eyes picked houses, ornamental shrubs, and trees out of the gloom. The northern New York, small-town version of suburbia gave up no clues as to where the blasted kid might be located.

Alan thought again about the weapon an informant

claimed Kenny was carrying. Kenny might be a punk 20-year-old kid, but his choice of firearm was definitely old-school.

A sawed-off, double-barrel, 12-gauge shotgun.

Loaded with solid-slug deer hunting loads, for the love of God.

The nervous chill of perspiration mingled with the damp air penetrating Alan's uniform. His bulletproof vest seemed to offer far too little coverage, only emphasizing how big a target his oversized body made.

Twenty yards to Alan's right, Deputy Jeff Sandil crouched with his Colt M-4 Carbine held at the ready. Covering Alan's backside, just like Alan was covering his.

Barely two minutes earlier, the joint drug task force raid on the crack operation in a nice little century-old Colonial-style house had gone spectacularly well – right up until Kenny took it into his most likely drug-riddled brain to dive out a window and make a run for it.

The kid had to be just ahead. Alan had glimpsed Kenny headed this way, before a hedgerow cut off visual contact.

When the sound of the fugitive's running footsteps then went silent, Alan figured Kenny must be hiding, catching his breath. Desperately trying to think, the way fugitives do when they're pushed into a corner.

Maybe plotting an ambush.

Alan eased his heavily-muscled, six-foot-two body around the hedgerow.

He silently crossed the empty blacktop driveway he found on the other side, his ears straining to pull any suspicious noise out of the air. The sound of a tractor-trailer shifting gears a quarter-mile away on Warren Street drifted on the cool, windless air. A door slammed somewhere behind him, probably one of the Glens Falls Police Department officers back at the crack house.

Stepping off the driveway onto a neatly trimmed lawn, Alan thought that all things considered, such as sawed-off shotguns, it might be nice to be nine miles farther north. There, he could be peacefully tracking down some interesting rumors he'd pumped out of another informant about illegal gambling in the Village of Lake George.

Then again, did he really want to give up a golden opportunity like this to finally throw Kenny Grisham in jail once and for all?

Jeff caught his eye, and signaled that he was ready to move on to the next house.

The hardnosed young deputy was relatively new to the department, having moved to Lake George only a year earlier, but he came with an excellent eight-year service record from the New York City Police Department.

Alan nodded to Jeff, and they moved into the next yard.

Alan scanned the landscaping around the Victorian home for likely hiding spots.

He saw a lot of them.

Alan's body moved forward with easy, dependable confidence over the dew-slicked lawn, unconcerned by any unease of the mind.

That physical grace and power had carried him with utter assurance to the finals of the NCAA Division I heavyweight wrestling championships two decades earlier.

Alan could recall all too well, however, how that match ended in a painful loss. A little unease might not have been a bad idea that night.

Now, he welcomed the roiling tightness growing in his gut, the breath racing in and out of his lungs. He told himself that fear is the best reminder a man has not to do anything stupid. A 12-gauge was a 12-gauge, no matter how hard he pushed his daily workouts these days to maintain his physical edge.

Glancing at Jeff, Alan suddenly spotted the barrel of a gun projecting from a tree next to the deputy. Alan snapped his Glock around, ready to fire.

The gun barrel resolved itself into a broken-off branch, clear enough in the gray twilight now that Alan took a better look. He let his breath out in a whoosh.

Jeff, body tense, more alert than ever, raised a questioning eyebrow.

Alan shook his head. He took a deep breath, and motioned the deputy forward again.

Damn Kenny anyway, Alan thought. Carrying a gun was a new wrinkle for the kid. Kenny had spent the last four years making himself a low-life thorn in the side of local law enforcement, Alan in particular. Never for anything serious, though.

Alan looked forward to seeing a nice weapons charge, not to mention Kenny's new association with crack dealers, change all that.

Maybe *this* time, Alan thought, Kenny's father, Carl Grisham, wouldn't be able to keep his son out of prison.

Back in high school, Alan thought of Carl as a major but basically harmless prick. Since then, Carl had surprised him by aggressively overachieving his way to the upper crust of the county's movers and shakers.

Alan shook his head and refocussed all his attention. He couldn't take time to gloat about Kenny yet. They still had to catch the kid.

As Alan scanned the shrubs tastefully arranged around the yard, the corner of his eye caught a hint of motion in a shadowy clump of small poplar trees behind Jeff.

Alan peered intently at the spot. He saw nothing but the vague grey darkness of tree trunks and leaves.

He kept looking. He'd seen *something* move. He wouldn't be satisfied until he knew what it was.

Jeff noticed Alan's stare, and started to turn.

The instant Jeff moved, a skinny form flashed into motion out of the trees.

No mistake this time. They'd spooked their prey into revealing himself.

The skinny figure held a stumpy object, that did indeed look for all the world like a sawed-off shotgun.

"There, going around the house!" Alan hollered, gesturing sharply, his Glock useless with Jeff in the line of fire.

The deputy dashed ahead as Kenny disappeared around the corner of the building. Alan considered himself a fast runner, but Jeff sprinted like this was the blasted Olympics.

Alan pushed himself hard, straining to catch up.

It crossed his mind that if any shooting broke out, his wife, Alice, and their kids, in his home only two streets over, would probably be able to hear the shots.

On the other hand, Kenny hadn't fired when he had the chance. Maybe the kid hadn't completely lost all common sense.

Jeff rounded the corner of the house, out of Alan's sight.

Alan heard Jeff's Brooklyn-accented command, "NYPD! FREEZE!"

Alan grinned at the deputy's adrenaline-pumped slip back into his old New York City jurisdiction.

Something to razz him about later, Alan thought, as relief that the chase was over this quickly welled up with unexpected intensity.

The gunshots squashed that hope.

A deep-throated **BOOM** that had to be Kenny's sawed-off echoed off the houses, freezing the grin on Alan's face.

A lighter **CRACK** from Jeff's M-4 Carbine and another heavy **BOOM** followed at machine-gun speed.

Jeff staggered back around the corner, almost colliding with Alan. Blood streamed down the deputy's sleeve. An acrid, sweet whiff of burnt gunpowder wafted around him.

"I'm okay," Jeff said, breathing hard. "Just nicked my arm. Vest took the other slug. Got off a shot. Don't think I hit him."

Alan hesitated. Jeff looked way too pale.

The deputy insisted, "Go on, get the bastard. I'll radio for backup."

Alan nodded. Readjusting his grip on his Glock, he carefully peeked around the corner. He saw Kenny 200 yards down the street, running in a hard panic sprint.

You better run, Alan thought. *God help you when I catch up.*

Kenny had stepped way over the edge into the big-time now. Alan felt ready, willing, and extremely able to show him exactly what that meant.

Carl Grisham could choke on his political connections trying to bail Kenny out of this one.

Holstering his Glock, Alan scooped up Jeff's M-4 and accelerated smoothly, a lion on the trail of a hyena. He kept the presence of mind to relax into his best running form.

The early morning twilight was brightening fast. A bad sign for Kenny.

The kid had a good lead, but Alan cut the distance in half by the time his prey darted across Warren Street.

The wail of a siren sliced through the air. Alan glanced back over his shoulder. Jeff stood far behind in the middle of the street, watching Alan and talking into his radio. Backup was on the way.

Kenny could still escape, though. Experience told Alan that Kenny not only possessed the morals of a weasel, but the instincts of one, too. The kid might panic easily, but those instincts would kick in sooner or later.

Alan loped across Warren Street. He closed the gap through a yard sloping down to one of the industrial sections of Glens Falls, home to the paper mill, limestone quarry, cement plant, the municipal waste treatment facility, vacant lots overgrown with trees and brush, and who knew what-all else these days.

Between two tractor-trailer trucks, the sun hung just on the horizon. Alan squinted against the sunrise shining redly in his eyes.

Kenny ducked around a semi.

Alan cursed and slowed. Losing sight of any suspect, let alone a cop-shooter armed with a 12-guage, is never a good idea.

Alan peered into the shadows under the truck.

No sign.

A dank, vaguely chemical odor surrounded him. Breathing deep but easily, he cautiously worked his way around the end of the truck.

Still no Kenny.

Alan felt the hair rising on the back of his neck.

This was not good at all.

Common sense belatedly said he'd pushed way too far on his own, ease off and wait for backup. He began reaching for his radio.

Alan froze when he heard the metallic *snick* of the action of a double-barrel shotgun being closed.

Like you'd hear after someone finally took the time to reload.

Every square inch of Alan's body not covered by his bulletproof vest seemed to become acutely sensitive. He realized, in particular, that Kenny was close enough to get damn good odds on a head shot.

"Drop the rifle, Alan," Kenny said. He panted from his run. His voice grated dryly, an old-man noise from a young throat. "Your handgun, too."

The adrenaline flooding Alan's system demanded action,

something, *anything,* as long as it was fast and hard.

Instead, he turned very slowly to stare down the stubby twin barrels of Kenny's sawed-off 12-guage.

"Kenny, if you were going to shoot me, you would have done it already," Alan said, daring to think he might still survive instead of dying on the spot.

"Maybe I need a live hostage, maybe I don't. Don't push me," Kenny said.

The 12-guage shook. The kid's bloodshot eyes revealed a stew of fear mixing with an angry, manic touch of crack.

Kenny leaned against the truck to steady the gun.

The blare of police sirens grew closer.

"Okay, Kenny, okay, just take it easy," Alan said. He slowly lowered Jeff's M-4 to the ground.

The semi's driver, nose buried in a manifest, came around the end of the truck and looked up. "What the...."

Kenny jumped. For a moment his gun waved indecisively between Alan and the driver.

Alan didn't hesitate. Moving with alarming quickness, he twitched the M-4 by the stock, swinging the barrel up to smack Kenny's right wrist.

The kid's sawed-off weapon fired a deafening blast and flew out of his hands at the same time.

Face twisted, Kenny threw a desperate punch at Alan's head.

Alan easily dodged the wild swing. He drove a fist into Kenny's stomach.

The kid hit the ground hard, doubled over.

Alan loomed over him, waiting for the thrill of victory to kick in.

Kenny didn't do anything, besides gasping and retching.

"Ah, hell," Alan muttered, several seconds later.

He took Kenny's wrists, far less roughly than many cops would have felt was necessary, and handcuffed him.

"I don't feel sorry for *you*, Kenny," Alan said. "You're smart enough to know what you were getting into. You do have a freakin' brain, or you did before you discovered drugs, anyway. I feel sorry for the man you *could have* been."

"*He* can go to hell," Kenny said, his eyes alive more than ever now with that angry, manic touch. "You can, too."

"The way you're going, you'll be there a lot sooner than me," Alan said.

He grabbed Kenny's shirt collar, stood the kid up with one hand, and started walking him to the GFPD patrol car that was pulling into the far end of the parking lot.

Alan looked back over his shoulder at the semi driver. "Thanks, buddy," he said. "Stick around. We're going to need a statement."

The driver, face pale, waved weakly with the hand that wasn't holding on to the truck for support.

Alan refocused on his captive.

"Want me to call your father for you, Kenny?" he said, raising his voice to be heard over the patrol car's blaring siren. "I'd be happy to give him the good news."

"You're going to love rubbing my old man's nose in this, aren't you?" Kenny said. He barked a brief, bitter laugh. "I can't blame you. He's an easy man to hate."

Kenny twisted around suddenly, bringing Alan to a halt. He lowered his voice so Alan could barely hear him over the siren.

"I tell you, dude, I wish to hell I'd taken a shot at my old man, instead of that damned cop."

Alan stared at him, for the first time in his life truly surprised by anything Kenny had to say.

Kenny smirked at the shocked expression on Alan's face, and laughed again. "Relax, McMendell. I'm just yankin' your chain."

Alan searched the depths of Kenny's bloodshot eyes, and

wasn't so sure.

The patrol car rolled to a stop next to them. Silence followed, as the Glens Falls patrol officer at the wheel, Bill Gantry, killed the siren.

"Nice work, Al," Bill said. He put a hand over his heart in mock dramatics. "Almost makes me sad you left the good ol' GFPD to sign on with the sheriff's department last year."

"Yeah, I tried to get out of Glens Falls," Alan said, matching Bill's dramatic tone, "but knuckleheads like Kenny here *just keep pulling me back in.*"

"Jeez, you need better material," Bill said, but he laughed anyway.

Alan laughed with him for a second. Then he mentally kicked himself for not remembering more important things sooner.

"Any word on Jeff Sandil?" he said.

"In the ambulance as we speak. Just a scratch on the arm. Possibly a couple cracked ribs. One of the slugs actually penetrated his vest. Luckily, it didn't hit him square."

"Ouch," Alan said. His own chest suddenly ached, as if remembering how Kenny aimed at it dead "square" with the sawed-off.

"Amen to that," Bill said. "On the other hand, your deputy was still making a pass at a female EMT, is what I hear over the radio."

"Glad to hear it."

"Yeah," Bill said, catching Alan's serious mood for a moment. It didn't last long.

"By the way, you'll never guess what we found in Kenny's crack house," Bill said.

"A half-pound of crack?"

"Looks like eight or nine ounces, yeah, but we knew about that going in. I mean something entirely different."

Alan kept silent as he deposited Kenny in the back seat of

the patrol car. He knew from his years in the GFPD that Bill would spill his guts soon enough, without any prodding.

"Gambling machines," Bill said. "You could outfit a freakin' casino with what we found."

Alan's head snapped around. The unexpected information took a little of the edge off the post-adrenaline-rush let down that was starting to make his hands shake.

Alan slammed the patrol car door shut, barely noticing how close the door came to crunching Kenny's elbow.

He gave Bill his full attention, ignoring the way his hands were now shaking like the proverbial leaves. "No kidding? Just a couple days ago I heard a rumor about an underground casino up in Lake George."

"Well, I'd say you might have a lead here," Bill said, studiously paying no attention to the condition of Alan's hands. "We found slots, a roulette wheel complete with rigging equipment, chips, decks of cards, the whole nine yards. Brand new, top-of-the-line stuff."

Alan absorbed this information, then gave Kenny a hard look.

"Casino equipment, Kenny? Are you gonna need Gamblers Anonymous to go with your drug rehab program?"

Kenny shrugged. "Don't look at me, dude. It's not *my* house."

"Whatsamatter, Kenny?" Bill said, grinning. "You didn't hear the damn politicians down in Albany still haven't even voted in casino gambling in Lake George, let alone in Glens Falls? Possession of unlicensed gambling equipment is a serious crime, kid."

Alan didn't think the charge quite measured up to drug dealing and the attempted murder of a police officer, but what the heck, he'd be happy to add it to Kenny's slate anyway.

Chapter 2.

Carl Grisham took a sip of his morning coffee in his usual downtown Glens Falls restaurant, Henry C's Cafe. Grisham was grayer than most 42-year-olds, medium height, and thin, like his son Kenny.

He wore an imported dark blue suit from Epczkha, a new, exclusive European designer label he doubted that few people in Glens Falls could even pronounce, let alone afford.

The tasteful, razor-sharp cut of the suit complemented the automatically haughty, *you better give me the respect I deserve* attitude in Grisham's gray-green eyes.

He restrained himself from shaking his head at the sight of the gray Dockers, plaid flannel shirt and beat up brown leather jacket worn by his guest, Charlie Payson.

A lean, brown-haired, blue-eyed six-footer, Payson sat on the other side of the table across the faded blue-and-white checked tablecloth.

Payson looked surprisingly fit for a computer nerd on the verge of middle age, but Grisham decided the man's taste in clothes hadn't improved any in the 20-some years since their days back in high school.

Putting Payson's non-existent fashion sense aside, Grisham considered strategy carefully. He expected no trouble siccing Payson on Alan McMendell, but he had to make sure.

It was *necessary* that Payson comply. Just thinking about McMendell brought violent fantasies spinning into Grisham's mind. The damned gall of the big son of a bitch, *striking* Kenny. Just like back in high school, McMendell seemed to think that being all huge and athletic gave him the right to do as he pleased.

Grisham had smacked Kenny around fair and square yesterday after moving heaven and earth to get him out on bail in record time. That was a *father's* right.

McMendell's police brutality, though, there was no way that could go unanswered.

Combine that with the way McMendell had started nosing around Grisham's Lake George interests, and Grisham had more than enough reason to put McMendell in Payson's crosshairs.

For a moment, the elegance of it struck Grisham – emotional need and practical benefit, two disparate forces, united toward a single goal. And McMendell betrayed by an old friend, Payson, to deliver the *coup de grace*.

If Payson did object to the role Grisham planned for him, well, Grisham possessed less elegant means to force compliance whether Payson liked it or not.

And, what the hell, Grisham decided he wouldn't mind sticking it to Payson, too.

The rising sun cast a blood-red glow through the gap between the three-story brick buildings across the street and into the big bay window of the cafe. Henry C's didn't officially start serving breakfast for another hour. They always opened early for Grisham, whenever he told them to.

When you're the banker who holds the mortgage over the cafe owner's head, you get perks.

The owner, Henry Crane, claimed to be a great grandnephew of Henry Crandall, the turn-of-the-20th-Century Glens Falls businessman and philanthropist. An early 1900's portrait of old Henry hung on the wall behind Grisham. Poster sized photos of Crandall Library and Crandall Park, parts of the legacy the old gentleman left to the community, adorned the other walls.

Grisham eyed the contemporary Henry, a portly, dark-haired man in his mid-30s, who was watching anxiously as Grisham took another sip of coffee.

Grisham noticed that the proprietor was actually holding his breath. Grisham paused, swishing the coffee in his mouth. He looked out the window, watching the sun climb up from the horizon.

"Acceptable," Grisham said at last. "I'm glad I didn't have to send it back, *again,* before you got it right."

Grisham smiled inwardly at the way Henry almost gasped as he began breathing again.

"Always glad to be of service, Mr. Grisham," Henry said.

On the other side of the table, Payson swallowed his coffee silently, offering neither complaint nor praise.

Grisham noticed, however, the glance that passed between Payson and Henry.

So, they knew each other. An interesting coincidence, if one believed in such things.

Grisham spared some thought to the potential ramifications, even though he was the one who initiated this meeting with Payson and had chosen the location himself.

Noticing Henry still hovering, Grisham waved him back into the kitchen.

"Don't interrupt us again," Grisham ordered.

"Of course not, sir," Henry said. He scurried away.

Grisham set his coffee mug down, and focused on Payson.

"Mr. Payson, I'd like to get right to the point. I want to...."

"Why so formal, Carl?" Payson said. "We're old acquaintances. Call me Charlie."

Grisham took a slow breath.

"All right, Charlie. As I was saying...."

"What's with this ungodly hour of the morning, Carlito? I should be home in bed."

Grisham felt his face flush. "Listen, people don't usually

interrupt me when I...."

"Now I'm remembering why we've hardly seen each other in twenty years," Charlie said. "Yeah, as I recall, you always had an excessively high opinion of yourself back in high school."

"Look who's talking," Grisham snapped. "You always thought you were the class brain."

"And I had the straight A's to prove it," Charlie said. He shrugged, and leaned back in his chair. "You set up this meeting, so *you* want something from *me*, not vice versa."

Grisham seized the retort on the tip of his tongue before the verbal lashing came out. He hadn't remembered Charlie being able to push his buttons like this. For all Payson's brains, he'd always struck Grisham as naive outside the classroom.

Whatever. Grisham could shift gears, if that's what took.

"The reason I set up meetings at this 'ungodly hour' is because I only need a couple hours of sleep. Dealing with people who are only half awake gives me an advantage."

"Ah, a little honesty," Charlie said. He raised an eyebrow. "How's that strategy been working out with me?"

Grisham made a show of sighing. "Point made, Charlie. You don't like being manipulated."

Charlie leaned forward. "I *can't* be manipulated, Carl."

Grisham smiled openly now. "We'll see," he said.

Grisham recalled that Charlie did have a competitive streak. In spite of his nerdiness, Charlie was a four-letter man on the wrestling team in high school, even made it to the state tournament his senior year, along with that big S.O.B. McMendell. That could be useful, aimed in the right direction.

"Charlie, I want...." Grisham paused, theatrically waiting a moment for Charlie to interrupt again. When Charlie remained silent, Grisham continued.

"I want you to take down Alan McMendell."

Charlie smiled blandly. "I'm a computer consultant, not a hit man."

"I said take him down, not take him out. You've known McMendell since kindergarten, and you're the best computer researcher in the business," Grisham said. There's nothing like flattering someone with the truth. "If anybody can dig up dirt on him, you're the man."

"My considerable skills notwithstanding, you know Alan and I are old friends."

"I know your 'old friend' tried to put you in prison last year."

Charlie looked out the window, and took another swallow of coffee.

"Alan's a professional. He was just following the evidence," Charlie said. He turned back to Grisham. "Evidence which turned out to be dead wrong, by the way."

"You exaggerate, Charlie. The evidence was never disproved. The grand jury simply decided there wasn't enough of it to charge you."

"If you want to get technical, I suppose."

"I'm a lawyer as well as a banker. We always get technical. And, *technically*, if more evidence were to happen to come along, the district attorney could still reopen the case."

Charlie's expression didn't change.

Grisham took that as a good sign. "Let's see, there were allegations of industrial espionage, and, what was the other thing? Oh yes, your best friend Brian Pierce was murdered. I believe he was McMendell's best friend, too."

Grisham shook his head, and continued. "Sad. Believe it or not, I actually liked Brian, in spite of the fact that he was friends with the two of you."

Charlie shifted in his chair. "Yeah, everybody liked Brian. But his murder was solv...."

"Yes, but there's been no explanation of how the drug dealer who killed him fit into an industrial espionage case."

Charlie's eyes narrowed. "Assuming there *was* any industrial espionage, you think you've got an explanation?"

Grisham handed over a sheet of paper.

Charlie read it quickly. "This is bull. A first-year law student could discredit it."

Grisham grinned expansively. "Maybe. It surely would pique McMendell's interest though, wouldn't it? Maybe lead him in, shall we say, an unfortunate direction?"

Charlie stood up. "If this is the best you can do, I'm outta here."

Grisham rose from his chair, still grinning. "Then let's get to the kicker. You're no ordinary computer consultant, are you, Charlie? I have a source who tells me you're one of the all-time great hackers."

Charlie's face lost all expression. "What idiot told you that?"

"An idiot who owes me big time. My goodness, given all the places he suspects you've hacked into, I'd say Alan McMendell could well be the least of your problems. How long do you think it would take the right federal agency to confirm, let's call it, your excess of curiosity?"

Grisham held Charlie with his eyes, and waited. This was indeed "the kicker" – whether the computer nerd would buy the argument, or figure out that Grisham was mostly blowing smoke, playing a bluff built from educated guesses based on vague hints extracted from his informant.

The stunned expression on Charlie's face encouraged Grisham.

Charlie waffled for a long few seconds, then slumped into his chair.

Grisham sat also, grinning wider than ever. "I always knew you were naive, Chuck. What made you think you could compete on my level?"

Charlie abruptly burst out laughing.

"Yeah, Carl," he said. The stunned look in his eyes disappeared. A calculating, even ruthless, calm replaced it. "I was naive back in high school. I'll give you that. A lot's happened since then."

Charlie leaned across the table. "If I were you, *Carlito,* I'd forget everything you just told me."

"And if I don't, *Chuck?*" Grisham remained calm. Now was when Charlie would try his own bluff, of course.

"If you don't," Charlie said, "I might just have to have a conversation of my own with my old semi-friend Investigator McMendell."

"You can't talk your way out of the evidence I have on you."

"A debatable point, but I can sure as hell talk him into the evidence I have on *you.*" Charlie's eyes glared into Grisham's. "About that idiot who owes you big time? Would that be a *gambling* debt?"

Grisham felt his hands closing into fists. Charlie couldn't possibly *know,* could he?

Charlie apparently noticed Grisham's reaction.

"Yeah, you're probably thinking I couldn't possibly know about your *casino* in Lake George, aren't you, Carl?"

"My what?"

Charlie snorted. "Give it up, man. You hid your connection to it pretty well, but I know all about the Grisham family's underground gambling casino. You know, the one your grandfather started way back during Prohibition."

Grisham stared. The cops hadn't been able to bust the casino for the better part of a century, and now Charlie Payson had blown open the secret in the single day since Grisham had summoned him.

"How...?" Grisham asked.

Charlie raised his hands, palms up. "When it comes to information, I do nice work."

Grisham urged his mind into gear again. Time for damage control. "So, I guess we have a stalemate."

"Guess so. The ol' Mexican stand-off, as one of my Marine squadmates would have called it."

"We should just go our separate ways then. No harm, no foul," Grisham said, trying to hide his surprise. The nerd had served in the freaking *Marines*?

"Actually, we're not quite finished," Charlie said. "There's one other bit of business I think we *can* conduct."

Grisham tried to read Charlie's expression. He sensed nothing more than general hostility. He took a deep breath.

"Go on."

"Henry Crane," Charlie said. "Man, you're some piece of work, Carl. Henry builds up a massive debt at your casino, then you let him mortgage his cafe to you, to pay off his gambling debt to you. And he doesn't even know the two are connected."

Grisham stiffened. "If you expect me to cancel Crane's debt...."

"Not at all. Debts need to be paid, although I *strongly* suggest you give Henry a very generous break on the interest rate. What I want you to do is cut him off at the casino."

"You mean bar him until he pays off his debt."

"Nice try. I mean bar him for life. Henry's got a problem with gambling, as I'm sure you know. It might still be early enough to put a stop to his addiction before he loses himself. I want your hooks out of him."

"In return, you'll provide me with information on McMendell?"

Charlie shook his head. "Dream on. I've got plans of my own for Alan, and they don't include you."

Charlie shifted his gaze to the front door, as if expecting

someone to walk in, then back to Grisham.

"Your next appointment is with a 'Mr. Smith,'" Charlie said. "You know, the organized crime guy who wants to horn in on your casino, if I'm not mistaken."

Grisham felt a hot flush of anger even as he cringed. Damn the man's intolerable nosiness! He tightened his self-control and said evenly, "What about this alleged Mr. Smith?"

"I'll give you all the intelligence I can find on him."

Grisham considered his options. As much fun as it was to grind Crane under his thumb, Smith *was* horning in on the casino. Information on him would be priceless. Charlie obviously knew it, too.

Grisham couldn't quite let go that easily.

"You're agreeing to keep quiet about my connection to the casino," he said. "That means you won't tell Crane, right?"

Charlie nodded knowingly. "You still need a concession from me, no matter how small. To save face."

Grisham shrugged. "Call it force of habit."

"I guess it's a small enough concession," Charlie said.

Grisham stood and put out his hand. "Done."

Charlie stood and shook hands, very firmly for someone who was supposed to be a computer geek.

He started turning to leave, then stopped.

"Oh, one more thing, Carlito."

Charlie's right hand shot across the table, grabbed Grisham by the hideously expensive Epczkha silk tie, and hauled him off balance until the two men were nose-to-nose.

"Don't ever call me 'Chuck' again."

Grisham bristled at the physical affront, and held his ground.

He glared straight back into Charlie's eyes, and said, "Don't ever call me 'Carlito' again."

Charlie actually smiled. "I think we have a deal."

Chapter 3.

Alan sat at his heavy metal desk in his office in the Sheriff's Department building next to the County Municipal Center. He abandoned his paperwork when Sheriff Ed Tellerman entered.

"Mornin' Al," said the sheriff.

Tellerman appeared to be about 50, with the wiry kind of build that comes from hiking the back woods of the Adirondack Mountains with a deer rifle for 40 years.

When Alan first met him, Tellerman gave the impression that he'd never been out of those back woods. The *magna cum laude* degree in civil engineering from Rensselaer Polytechnic Institute hanging on the sheriff's office wall argued otherwise. Over the last year, Alan had seen Tellerman deftly slice and dice the bullshit spouted by suspects as well as by the occasional county supervisor wanting to cut the Sheriff's Department budget.

"Sir," Alan said, standing to greet his superior.

"You gotta get over this formality, Al. Call me Ed, and sit down, for Chrissake."

"Normally I would, but we both know this isn't a social visit."

The sheriff nodded. "You musta seen Carl Grisham's lawyer comin' to my office."

"Yeah. I didn't think he'd be wasting any time, after the way he got Kenny out yesterday. Didn't think he'd be here at seven freaking a.m., though."

"I gave him the idea you were up in Lake George, 'cause I wanted to talk to you first. When he catches up to you, he's gonna serve you with a subpoena. Grisham's launchin' a civil suit charging you deprived his son of his civil rights."

Alan sighed, and sat back in his chair. "I'm surprised he didn't try for a criminal charge first."

The sheriff took the room's other chair. "I think 'concurrent' is the lawyer-speak for it. He's also pushin' the D.A. to indict you for police brutality."

"And the D.A. says...?"

"Look, you and Joe Hanrahan aren't buddies, but we both know he's not the kinda guy to fold under political pressure. He'll go with the evidence. Just like you."

"So, in theory, I've got nothing to worry about."

At least not on the criminal angle, Alan thought. But Grisham's lawyer was the best money could buy. Who knew what a great lawyer could get a jury to believe in a civil suit?

Alan abruptly slammed the heel of his hand against his heavy metal desk. The desk grated a foot across the floor. It bumped against the sheriff's chair.

"Sorry," Alan muttered. He quickly yanked the desk back. Ed eyed him coldly.

"Rearrange the furniture all ya want," he said, "but I think you better stay away from Grisham."

Alan opened his mouth to protest, then caught himself before the flood of words came out.

"Sure," he said instead. "As long as I don't dig up any evidence that points in his direction."

A large part of the coldness left the sheriff's expression. "Any chance of that?" he said.

"I wish, Ed. I wish." Alan felt his muscles tightening, as if his body really, seriously wanted to hit the desk again.

The sun, just high enough in the morning sky to lose its reddish tinge, cast a cheerful yellow light into Henry C's Cafe. Grisham sat with his back to the window, facing Mr. Smith.

The meeting with Smith was going well enough, so far, even though the early morning hour didn't seem to affect Smith any more than it had affected Charlie Payson.

Grisham hated to admit it, but the keyed-up mental edge forced into his mind by his confrontation with Payson might have actually helped in dealing with the mob chieftan.

Smith didn't fit what Grisham thought of as the old-time organized crime cliches. Somewhere in his mid 30's, blond hair, no expensive suit, no bent nose. The yuppie-style casual clothes didn't fool Grisham, though, and he figured Smith must have underlings who got *their* noses bent on his behalf.

Or else Smith was the one who committed the bending. The man certainly looked capable of bending just about anybody. He might even be bigger than Alan McMendell.

Grisham extended his hand across the table. "I take it we have a deal, Mr. Smith?"

Smith looked at Grisham's hand as though contemplating the best way to squash a cockroach. Then he reached out and took Grisham's hand in an iron grip.

"We got a deal. When we get the state to finally legalize casino gambling here in Lake George, we'll be looking for your behind-the-scenes work to grease the skids with the local governments." His grip tightened. "Don't disappoint us."

"Just convince those halfwit legislators in Albany," Grisham said. "I'll hold up my end."

"Of course you will," Smith said, tightening his grip yet again, to emphasize that this was a command, not a compliment. "In the meantime, be extra careful with our casino up on the lake."

Grisham carefully hid the way Smith's use of the word "our" grated. The Grisham family casino had always been an independent operation. Until Smith.

"I've got a rock solid informant in the Sheriff's

Department," Grisham said. "Any hint of a raid, we'll know."

Smith did nothing, other than maintaining the power of his grip on Grisham's hand.

"We've never been raided," Grisham said. His hand ached as if the bones were about to crack, but he kept his voice steady. "Staying way ahead of the law runs in my family."

Smith nodded, but his eyes remained unimpressed.

"I got informants of my own I can activate," he said. "You'll have to up my percentage of the gross, though."

Grisham ground his teeth silently, wondering for the thousandth time why the hell he never put up any resistance when Smith "suggested" that he accept Smith's "assistance" with the casino, back when there might have been some slim chance of keeping the man out of it.

For the thousandth time, the answer came back – Smith represented a shot at the legalized casino motherlode. There was no way Grisham could pass up the chance for a share of *that,* could he?

Especially not now, with the state governor backing it – gotta compete for those tourism dollars – and the legislature about to consider expanding the reach of the amendment to the state constitution that allowed full-blown, off-reservation, non-Indian casinos in selected locations.

It crossed Grisham's mind that with legal casinos on the line, it might be smart to shut down his gambling house for the time being, even though there was no telling how long it would take the halfwit legislators to act.

Grisham dismissed the police in contempt, even after Kenny's moronic stunt handed them the new equipment Grisham had acquired for updating the casino. The stuff was untraceable.

Still, there was always a chance McMendell or some other cop might stumble onto something out of sheer dumb luck. Not to mention the small but real risk of Charlie Payson turning into a loose cannon. It wouldn't do to stir up the populace with the publicity that would surround the bust of a major illegal gambling operation.

The Lake George casino was a gold mine, though, the proverbial license to print money. Nothing compared to what legalized gambling would bring, but way too much tax-free income to give up, even with Smith now taking a cut.

The core of the Lake George summer season was coming on, too. All those tourists, just aching to be separated from their money.

"We're not quite done, Grisham," Smith said, interrupting Grisham's mental calculation of the summer's likely net proceeds. "Your son Kenny cost us a bundle getting all that new equipment confiscated. That is, he cost *you* a bundle."

Grisham actually felt himself relaxing. He was wondering why this particular axe hadn't fallen. Now that it had, he could handle it. If Smith wanted only money, that could always be arranged.

"Understood, Mr. Smith."

"Good. And Kenny needs to be...."

"I've dealt with my son," Grisham said quickly. Maybe a little too quickly. He kicked himself for interrupting Smith, but the mob boss might've been about to say something Grisham couldn't risk allowing to be said out loud. "I promise you, Kenny won't cause any more trouble."

"You better be right. If not, *I'll* be the one dealing with the both of you."

Before Grisham could reply, a sharp *snap!* of breaking glass came from the window behind him, almost simultaneously with the sound of the gunshot out on the street.

Smith's head jerked.

A red flow of blood appeared on his temple.

Smith's grip convulsively tightened even more on

Grisham's hand, finally forcing a gasp out of the smaller man.

"Grisham, if you set me up...." Smith's voice slurred into silence. His iron grip slackened to rust, and faded to nothing as he toppled out of his chair.

Alan controlled his urge to do damage to his office furniture. Then he grinned at the sheriff as another thought occurred to him.

"Of course," Alan said, "we haven't even started to talk about my *real* problem."

"What now?" Ed said, looking at him quizzically.

"Well, I still have to break this Grisham lawsuit news to Alice."

"Oh, yeah. Wives!" Ed said, grinning back. "Ya never know how they're gonna react."

The intercom on Alan's phone beeped.

"Alan, Bill Gantry on line two," said the deputy on the other end of the line.

"Hold on a minute."

"Take it," the sheriff said, standing up to leave. "We're done for now."

"Thanks," Alan said.

He stabbed the "line two" button with a finger and picked up his phone.

"Bill! What's goin' on.... No kidding...." Alan felt his grin widening as he listened to Bill's story. Carl Grisham, involved in a shooting? This was way too good to be true.

"*What?*" Alan said, his grin fading as Bill went on. "*Innocent bystander?* Bill, gimme a break.... Henry Crane backs him up? Hell.... *Charlie Payson?* What about him.... Uh, yeah, sure. I'll be glad to talk to him. Although, maybe I should talk to him alone.... Yeah, you'll be the first to know how it goes."

Alan hung up the phone gently, resisting the urge to give it the same treatment he gave his desk.

It was bad enough that the one piece of potentially good news he'd heard about Grisham in years probably wasn't going to amount to anything.

Now, he and *Charlie Payson* were going to cross paths again.

God Almighty, Alan thought. *As if I don't have enough problems.*

The Adirondack Northway, Route 87, above the Village of Lake George.

Chapter 4.

Alan stood next to Charlie Payson in the living room of the apartment Charlie used as an office, in a relatively new house on one of the higher back streets in the Village of Lake George.

Alan studied Charlie without trying to hide the fact that he was doing so. Alan felt his breath coming quicker as he psyched himself up for the coming encounter. If past experience was any guide, attempting to pry information out of his old one-time friend would be no easy task.

Assuming, of course, that Charlie had anything to do with the shooting of Mr. Smith that morning.

All Alan knew so far was that the GFPD turned up a witness who saw Charlie leaving Henry C's shortly before Smith took the bullet.

It would be...interesting...to hear Charlie's explanation.

Alan stalled for a long moment, taking in the view out Charlie's window – a tree-lined village street under the mid-morning sun. Through a gap between two 70-foot-tall sugar maples, Alan caught a glimpse of the southern basin of Lake George, the blue water of the lake itself.

The sound of traffic screaming by on Interstate 87, the Adirondack Northway, infiltrated from uphill. The noise was surprisingly low, partially muffled by the strip of trees and brush holding down the embankment separating the six-lane highway from the residential street.

Alan turned to the row of half a dozen laptop computers lining a table on one side of Charlie's living room. The display began with a primitive Tandy 1800HD from the early 1990's. Alan remembered seeing how excited Charlie was after his parents gave him the Tandy for Christmas all those years ago, laughable though its capabilities were by modern standards.

From there, Charlie's collection progressed in sophistication up to what was undoubtedly the latest, fastest, multi-Mega-Giga-whatever-warpspeed model available. Alan could even smell the just-out-of-the-box, new-electronics odor hanging in the room.

Just about every laptop Charlie ever owned must be there, Alan thought.

He did a double-take at the sight of one of the more recent models. Its casing was battered into a thousand cracks, and riddled with .45-caliber bullet holes.

"Charlie, how the hell did you get your hands on that?" Alan demanded. "It's supposed to be in the county evidence locker!"

"Don't worry, my original is still there, as far as I know," Charlie said. He grinned. "I smashed and shot this one myself, as close to the final condition of my original as I could remember. Not as meaningful as the real one, of course, but I couldn't leave a gap in my collection, could I?"

"I suppose not, if you want to be that way about it." Alan took his eyes off the mangled computer and faced Charlie. "I

Charlie's Tandy 1800HD laptop computer. Front-line technology, circa 1992, with 1 megabyte of RAM (expandable to 3), a 20-megabyte hard drive, 12 megaHertz clock speed, 3 1/2 inch floppy drive, and MS-DOS 5.0.

wonder what Brian would have to say about you wanting to keep that as a momento, considering the price he paid."

Charlie's grin disappeared. "He wouldn't think anything about it. He was already dead by the time my laptop bit the dust."

"Yeah, I know that part all too well."

Charlie bent over the damaged machine, apparently examining the computer's broken hard drive through one of the bullet holes.

"Alan, I don't have anything more to say about Brian now than I did in front of the grand jury a year ago," he said. "If you're just here to dredge the up the past, get out."

"Mighty touchy about that, aren't you? Okay, I'll let it go.

For the time being. Right now, actually, I want you to explain something else."

"Sure," Charlie said. He straightened up and walked into the apartment's kitchen. "Orange juice? Milk?" he added, opening a well-stocked fridge.

"No thanks," Alan said, following him and squeezing his bulk into a chair at the kitchen table.

"Maybe a beer?" Charlie said.

"At this hour of the morning? Besides, I'm on duty."

"Is that so?" Charlie said, grabbing an ice tray out of the freezer and vigorously twisting it to crack loose a couple of cubes. "Well, I'm always happy to cooperate with law enforcement."

Alan snorted. "Since when?"

Charlie laughed. "Well, cooperate within the bounds of police authority and my Constitutional rights. In my experience, if you give the authorities more than they're entitled to, it doesn't take very long for them to start thinking they *are* entitled to it."

Charlie put his ice cubes in a glass, and poured orange juice over them. He sat down across the table from Alan.

"So," Alan said, "how's Helen?"

Charlie nodded. "I see we're going for a little more misdirection before getting to the point. Well, why not? My wife is visiting her mother over in Pilot Knob."

"She'll be back soon?"

Charlie looked out the window. "It's an extended visit."

"Oh. I see," Alan said. "She's left you."

Charlie started to protest, then sighed.

"It's only fair, I suppose," Charlie said. "I divorced Helen once, as you no doubt recall. I came back, though, so maybe she will too."

"To tell you the truth," Alan said, "I'm not sure why she took you back."

Charlie laughed softly for a second. "You and me both."

"So, what's this latest dustup about?"

Charlie shrugged. "I can be a bit much to take in long exposure. She'll be back when that effect wears off."

Charlie's expression grew serious. "And, on that note, detective, let's dispense with the misdirection and get down to it. You have questions. Fire way."

"Charlie, where were you around six o'clock this morning?"

Charlie examined Alan's face, and smiled. "Why don't you tell me?"

"My friends in the GFPD...."

"They're still friends with you, even after the way you ditched them to join the sheriff's department?"

"Some people know what real friendship means, Charlie."

"You're saying I don't? I was a good friend to Brian, and I am to you, no matter what you think."

"I thought we weren't talking about Brian."

Charlie paused, but only for a fraction of a second.

"You were saying?" he said. "About your friends in the GFPD?"

"You were seen leaving Henry C's in Glens Falls early this morning, shortly before a Mr. Smith was shot at the cafe."

Alan couldn't tell whether Charlie wasn't surprised to hear about the shooting, or whether he was just trying to project an in-control image. Whichever, Charlie kept his cool.

"So, you want to know if I killed this guy?" he said.

"Who said anything about a killing?" Alan said, watching Charlie as carefully as only a veteran cop knows how. "The victim is very much alive at Glens Falls Hospital."

Charlie didn't falter for even a millisecond.

"That must be good news for all concerned," he said.

"Everyone except the shooter."

"And you're wondering if that would be me?"

Alan shrugged, in a way that emphasized the massive build of his shoulders. "Or, if you might have seen something that could be helpful."

"How nice. I'm being given the benefit of the doubt," Charlie said. He leaned forward. "Believe me, Al, if I was going to shoot anyone in that cafe, it would've been Carl Grisham, not some huge guy I never met."

"So, you were at the cafe. With Grisham, of all people."

"Before the gunplay, yeah, just like your old GFPD buddies told you, I'm sure. Grisham had a business proposition for my consulting firm."

"He conducts business at six a.m.?"

"Sometimes, apparently. You remember what a horse's ass he was in high school. He hasn't changed a bit." Charlie grinned again. "What am I saying? The way you and Grisham have gone at each other about his kid, you know what the big wiener is like better than I do."

Alan grinned too. This was just like old times, when he and Charlie and Brian used to hang out together. Before Charlie came back a year ago from whatever the hell computer company job he had in California.

Before Brian ended up dead.

"So, you're consorting with the enemy now, consulting for Grisham?" Alan said.

"Give me a break, man. His proposition didn't interest me."

The answer killed Alan's briefly nostalgic mood. It took him a moment to figure why.

"That's not exactly the truth, is it?" he said.

Charlie didn't seem to take offense. "On the contrary, it's precisely the truth."

"Okay, then it's not the whole truth. What is it you're leaving out?"

Charlie's grin never dimmed. "Careful, Al. Somebody

might accuse you of getting perceptive in your old age."

"In a minute, somebody's going to accuse me of losing my patience," Alan said, rising out of his chair.

Charlie lost the grin, but didn't back down.

"By the way," Charlie said, "Very nice job. Bringing up Brian, trying to use him to knock me off balance, put me off guard. Who's being a good friend now?"

Alan very slowly reached across the table to Charlie's untouched glass, and chugged the orange juice in a couple of swallows.

Then he slammed the glass down on the table, and at least got the satisfaction of seeing Charlie jerk back.

"Charlie, you remember when we were on the wrestling team back in high school?" Alan said.

"What's this, an appeal to sentimentality?"

"It's a warning, my friend. I always beat you when we faced off in our practice matches."

"The way I remember it, I held my own."

"I didn't say it was easy. I always won in the end, though."

"Only on the mats, Al."

"Just keep telling yourself that."

Alan left Charlie in the kitchen and was already out the apartment's front door when Charlie stopped him on the tiny porch.

"You're always going to blame me for Brian's death, aren't you?" Charlie said.

Alan turned impatiently. What the hell was Charlie's point?

"Why shouldn't I blame you?" Alan said. "You blame yourself."

Charlie smiled sadly and shook his head. "I'm not the one who hasn't forgiven himself," he countered.

Alan opened his mouth, ready to snap back, *Oh, I suppose you have.*

The thought stopped him cold.

The galling, unthinkable implication hung in the air.

Charlie *had* forgiven himself.

Alan stared at his one-time friend, struggling to find a response that didn't involve taking Charlie's head off.

Charlie, perhaps realizing how far he'd pushed, closed the door in Alan's face.

But slowly.

Alan could have replied, could have stopped the door. Could have stepped back inside and pounded Charlie into the floor with the SOB's favorite laptop computer.

Alan just stood instead, watching the door close until he heard the latch click into place.

He briefly debated whether to knock on the door, or perhaps kick it down.

Then, he took a deep, calming breath, let it out slowly, and began walking back to his car.

Damn, he should have known better than to try to get the last word in with Charlie. Back in high school, Brian was the only one who could pull that off, and only about half the time at that.

Of course, back then it was all in fun. Back then, Charlie knew better than to nail his friends with painful truths. Not that there were many painful truths in those carefree days when they all thought they would live forever.

Climbing into his car, Alan took another deep breath, and dared to ask himself the question.

Did he blame himself for Brian's death?

Yeah, of course he did.

His guilt wasn't as direct as Charlie's, but there it was. If he'd been with Brian and Charlie that night, as he should have been....

Alan started the car, and forced his mind to return to the present.

That's when he began to wonder how long it would take Charlie to realize that he had accurately described someone he'd "never met" as a "huge guy."

Then he wondered if Charlie knew all along.

Chapter 5.

Mr. Smith regained a foggy sense of consciousness in the intensive care unit at Glens Falls Hospital. He sensed an incredibly young, and rather pleased looking intern. The doctor seemed insistent on shining a flashlight in Smith's eyes.

"You're right on schedule, Mr. Smith," the intern said. "I had ten thirty in the ICU pool, and here you are waking up at ten twenty-nine. That's a mighty tough skull you've got."

When Smith looked at him as if sizing up a Martian, the young doctor sighed. He eased into a more businesslike bedside manner.

"You're in the hospital, Mr. Smith. I'm Dr. Moden. You were struck in the head by a bullet earlier this morning. Lucky for you, it didn't hit you squarely."

"What? Who the frigging hell did it?" Smith said. His voice came out a harsh croak. He suddenly realized he was terribly thirsty.

Dr. Moden smiled. "I don't know, but I wouldn't worry, Mr. Smith. The police are just outside. Nobody but hospital staff can get to you."

Smith glared. "I'm the one lying here with a bullet hole in the head, and you want me to depend on the cops?"

Smith struggled to sit up. The doctor put out a restraining hand.

"Please relax, Mr. Smith. The bullet didn't penetrate your skull, but you might have a mild concussion. You should try to avoid getting excited."

"What happened?" Smith said.

"Well, I don't know how official this is, but from what I hear, you were having breakfast at a cafe when a bullet came through the window and hit you. We hardly ever ever get gunshot wounds around here. You and the police officer shot in that drug raid a couple days ago are the talk of the hospital."

Noticing Smith's glare gaining intensity, the intern got to the point. "There's been some street gang activity starting up in the area, unfortunately. And to think I moved to this small-town area to get away from that sort of thing. Anyway, from what I hear, the police are leaning toward the 'stray bullet from gang-related violence' theory."

Smith allowed himself to drop back onto the pillow.

Stray bullet, my ass, he thought. In his experience, people got shot for a reason. Usually *his* reason.

Shaking off the anesthesia fog in his brain faster than the young punk of a doctor would have thought possible, Smith asked for some water and a phone.

"Certainly," the intern said, pouring a glass of water and holding the straw to Smith's lips. "Like I said, the police are outside, though. They want to ask you a few questions as soon as possible."

Smith stopped sipping. "Me? I was minding my own business in a cafe. What do they need to ask me?"

"I'm sure it's just routine. They have procedures they have to follow for any gunshot wound."

"I need to make a phone call first," Smith said.

He thought he saw the doctor's eyes begin to narrow. Smith exerted his willpower, and produced a smile for the snot-nosed little shit.

"Gotta let the wife know I'm okay," he said. "If you're married, you must know how that goes."

Smith watched the intern's face relax.

"Yeah, I guess you're right," the young doctor said. "If I

got shot and my wife was the last to know, I'd never hear the end of it."

Smith forced himself to chuckle appreciatively.

The intern put the room's phone on the bedside stand within Smith's reach.

"I'll tell the officers, what, maybe ten minutes? If you need anything else, just holler."

"You bet," Smith said, still holding his smile. "Thanks. By the way, how long before I can get out of here?"

"We'd like to keep you overnight for observation, make sure your brain keeps firing on all cylinders, so to speak. Barring the unlikely complication, you should be out of here tomorrow. Like I said, you've got one tough skull."

After the doctor left, Smith raised his eyes to the ceiling. Local cops! His life would be so much better if the police in this Godforsaken backwater never so much as saw him, even if he did have a good cover story.

Well, that's what cover stories were for, and his was prepared by the best – himself. It was certainly adequate to fool these backwoods hicks.

Smith took a few more swallows of water.

His head wound began to throb.

He gripped the telephone receiver hard enough to make the plastic creak.

He needed information, and he knew how to get it.

Screw Dr. Moden.

Screw the damn local cops, too.

He'd been *shot*.

Somebody had to pay.

Smith began making calls.

Canada Street, the main drag in the Village of Lake George.

Chapter 6.

Henry Crane locked the back door of Henry C's for the night and climbed into the rusty hulk of his '89 Chevy S-10 Blazer. Its old V-6 thrummed to life with only a small belch of blue smoke out the exhaust.

Henry drove purposefully north on Glen Street. He picked up Gloria, the woman he hoped would become his new girlfriend, at her house on Glen, just across from Crandall Park.

Then he kept going north, headed for Exit 19 of the Northway.

He knew exactly where he wanted to go.

At Exit 19, Henry got on the northbound lane, taking the fastest route to the underground casino in Lake George.

"How crazy is my life going to get, anyway?" he asked Gloria, secretly glad to have some exciting news to tell her.

A man *shot* in his cafe! Police all over the place. He told Gloria all about that.

He didn't tell her about how Carl Grisham, thank God he was there, explained before the cops arrived exactly what Henry should say. Henry made damn sure he got the story straight, so he wouldn't let Mr. Grisham down.

Speaking of not letting him down, Henry had lost a full day's business in the bargain, with more losses to come if the police didn't let him reopen soon. With a mortgage payment to Mr. Grisham coming up, and his "other debts," as he called his current losses at the casino, this was no time for a cash flow problem.

Henry felt oddly buoyant, though, anticipating his evening at the casino. With all this bad luck raining down on him in one lump sum, his fortunes had to change.

Already were changing, he reminded himself. He was out on his first date with Gloria, the best-looking woman he'd ever worked up the courage to ask, wasn't he?

No doubt about it, tonight was going to be his night.

He recalled his first casino gambling experience a couple months back, at the Oneida Indian Nation's Turning Stone Casino between Utica and Syracuse.

He could *almost* relive the unbelievable charge of winning that $50,000 jackpot at the slots, like nothing he'd ever felt before. He paid off the mortgage on Henry C's with that windfall.

The mortgage he had back then, anyway. He thought he lucked out when a friend hooked him up with the Lake George casino, but this streak of bad luck had been dogging him ever since. It forced him to take out another mortgage to cover his losses.

Carl Grisham had been a real godsend at the bank, helping line up the new loan. Henry knew he'd have no trouble repaying Mr. Grisham when his luck came back, which had to be any time now.

Yes, his friend Charlie kept nagging him to quit, had even started telling him he had a "problem." For a really smart guy, Charlie apparently didn't understand how luck worked.

Henry knew the Lake George casino was absolutely illegal, of course. He wondered whether he would miss that particular part of the thrill, when and if casino gambling was ever legalized in the Lake George region.

For now, though, he could imagine himself some 1920s "swell," taking his "Flapper" girlfriend to a speakeasy for a night of genteel wagering and sipping Prohibition bootleg hootch.

Henry parked the Blazer on the next street west from Canada Street, the main drag in the Village of Lake George. He and Gloria picked their way past the dumpster in back of a squat, apparently vacant commercial building.

Henry knocked on the signless door.

The doorman recognized Henry, depriving Henry of the ritual of exchanging passwords. The man, his relentlessly average 40-something looks matched by the generic name of Joe, was so unimaginative he didn't even bother escorting Henry and Gloria to the stairs.

The casino existed underground literally as well as legally. Henry and Gloria descended the steps to the basement.

Henry's pulse quickened at the sights and smells rising to greet them at the bottom. The odors of beer and human bodies swirled around, like they did at any bar, modern or 1920s.

Cigarette and cigar smoke, like you didn't find in regular bars these days, hung so thick you could build an outhouse out of it.

Bright lights dangled pools of illumination over tables of card players, a row of slots, and the centerpiece of the room, a roulette wheel.

The lights left the basement's dingy concrete walls in shadow, out of sight and out of mind.

The crowd was a little sparse, but it was early yet.

Henry bounded forward, oblivious to Gloria's smoke-fueled cough.

"How about the roulette wheel?" Henry asked.

Gloria rallied, bringing her coughing under control. This was her first date with Henry. He might be a little on the chubby side, but he was kinda cute, and she was 35. Her biological clock was ticking at an increasingly alarming volume these days. She wasn't about to give up on the date that easily.

"Sounds good to me," she said.

Henry, playing the 1920s gentleman, held Gloria's chair for her, then seated himself.

"Hey, Henry," said Jason, the blond, college-age kid spinning the wheel. "Where you been lately?"

Henry grinned at him. "Out finding the love of my life. Jason, meet Gloria."

Jason eyed Gloria up and down in appreciation. "Too good for the likes of you, Henry," he pronounced.

Gloria blushed. "Thank you, Jason."

Henry smacked $20 down on the table. "Just watch the wheel, sonny," he said in mock indignation. "And put that twenty on black." A relatively safe bet, just to test the waters.

"Yowsa, boss," Jason said.

Jason spun the wheel, and sent the little ball racing around its track. It eventually rattled to a stop.

"Twenty-seven black!" Jason said. "My man Henry's starting the evening right."

Henry's smile outshone the overhead lights. He looked into Gloria's warm, excited eyes, and gave her hand a gentle squeeze.

"They ain't seen nothing yet, kiddo," he said.

Yes indeed, his luck was finally changing.

From across the room, what might almost have been a smile crossed the face of pit boss Frank Banfield as he watched Jason working the customers at the roulette wheel.

The kid had the touch, no doubt about it. None of Frank's other employees could shmooze the marks, uh, *customers,* the way Jason could, making them feel good while getting clipped.

The customer Jason was currently shmoozing turned his head, giving Frank his first good view of the man. The almost-smile on Frank's face got scared away by the scowl that replaced it.

Henry Crane. Christ, how the hell had he gotten in? Then Frank remembered. Joe arrived late for work. Frank hadn't gotten around to relaying the word from on high that Crane was now blacklisted.

Henry was deeply engrossed in explaining roulette strategy to Gloria, when he felt a hand on his shoulder.

He looked up and smiled. "Frankie! You're just in time to see me win back what I owe you."

The pit boss smiled pleasantly. "Mr. Crane, could you come with me for a minute? There's something we need to discuss."

"Couldn't we do it later? I'm on a roll here."

"I would prefer now," Frank said. His smile remained pleasant.

Henry felt the pit boss's hand on his shoulder start to squeeze. Hard.

"Take it easy, Frank," Henry said, standing. "If it's all that important, sure."

"Jason," Frank ordered. "Whatever his lady friend wants. On the house."

"Absolutely, boss."

Henry looked back at Gloria as the pit boss walked him to the office at the end of the room. The confused look in her eyes gave him a sinking feeling in the pit of his stomach.

Frank closed the office door behind them.

"You've been a good customer, Henry, so I'm doing this in private, instead of in front of your girl. You've been barred."

The building's foundation seemed to tilt under Henry.

"What?" he said.

"I think you know what 'barred' means."

"But...why? If it's about my tab, c'mon, you know I'm good for it."

"I didn't bring you in here to debate." The expression in Frank's eyes grew hard. "The owner says you're barred. Collect your girl and go."

"No!" Henry said, waving a finger in the pit boss's face.

They couldn't take this away from him, not when he finally had Gloria, not when every sign said his good luck was back. Not when he had so much riding on making a good score.

"Careful, Henry," Frank said.

"I know what this is really about," Henry said, ignoring the warning tone in Frank's voice. "It's because I started winning for a change, isn't it?"

"Out. Now," Frank said.

"No! You can't dismiss me like some nobody," Henry said, his voice rising. He grabbed the pit boss's lapels. "I'm right, aren't...."

Henry never even saw the fist that slammed into his solar plexus, driving him to his knees, bent over and gasping.

The pit boss loomed over him. "Crane, I do you the courtesy of avoiding embarrassing you in front of your girl, and this is how you repay me?"

It occurred to Henry that what Frank really wanted to avoid was punching out a customer in front of the other customers.

He heard a knock on the office door.

"We're done, Crane," Frank said, turning away from him and opening the door.

"No!" Henry said. He had to make the pit boss understand. He lurched to his feet and grabbed Frank's shoulder to spin him around.

Henry saw the fist this time, a blur homing in on his left cheek bone, but what really caught his attention was the sight of Gloria standing behind Jason in the doorway.

Then his world exploded into pain and bright lights.

The next thing he remembered was hearing Jason's voice saying, "Wow!"

Henry blearily opened his eyes a tiny slit. The pit boss was standing over him, rubbing his knuckles. Jason stood beside him, goggle-eyed. Henry caught only a glimpse of Gloria, mostly hidden behind Jason.

Henry thought her eyes looked disappointed.

He let his own eyes close. He couldn't face Gloria like this. And, let's face it, he was scared to face Frank, too. A man he thought was his friend just two minutes earlier.

Henry felt a foot jab him in the leg. Henry didn't move.

He heard Jason saying, "Man, out cold."

Then Frank's voice. "Well, miss? You want to wait for him to come around?"

"No." Gloria's voice. Frightened. Embarrassed. "I want to go home."

Henry's heart shriveled.

"Randy!" Frank's voice, shouting out into the casino. "Get

this lady to a cab."

Then the door closed, shutting out the sounds of gamblers enjoying a good time.

"Well, Jason?" Frank's voice again, patient, but edged with a touch of menace. "Why aren't you at the roulette wheel?"

"That's what I came to tell you, boss," Jason said. "The wheel's on the fritz again. The rigging mechanism's totally out of whack this time."

Henry cringed inwardly. *Rigging mechanism?* Charlie had tried to warn him the place was a rip-off, but he hadn't listened.

They're all my friends at the casino, Henry had explained. *They wouldn't do that to me.*

Gods, how freaking naive could a man be?

Maybe Gloria was right to leave him lying here.

Frank's voice, still grilling Jason. "That doesn't explain why you brought the woman."

Henry could almost hear Jason hanging his head.

"Sorry, boss. I guess I didn't realize the lady was following me."

"Awareness, kid. Listen to me. You gotta develop that in this business."

"Right, boss." Jason paused, then added, as if thinking out loud, "This never would have happened if the owner's kid hadn't gotten the new equipment confiscated. Screwing around with crack, even shooting a cop. What an idiot."

Frank's voice, now a mix of menace and exasperation. "Quiet about that. Crane's right here on the damned floor."

A hint of fear could be heard in Jason's voice now.

"Easy, boss. Look."

Henry felt a foot smash into his shin. He strangled the cry of pain trying to burst out of his mouth, and didn't move a muscle.

"See?" Jason again. "Out cold."

The pit boss grunted. "Okay, this time. You got the gift of gab, kid, but you gotta learn when to keep your mouth shut."

"Right, boss."

"Damn straight I'm right. Now stay here, and get this loser out of here when he comes around."

Henry only half listened to Frank's departure. A simple question consumed his mind.

How Goddamned fucking naive could a man be?

The news media had gone nuts the day before, reporting the drug bust and the gambling equipment confiscated along with the crack, and, of course, Carl Grisham's son, Kenny, shooting a cop.

That meant that *Carl Grisham* was the owner of the Lake George casino.

Mr. Grisham, the ever-helpful banker, always looking out for Henry's best interests.

What a joke.

Grisham was, in truth, the cause of all Henry's problems.

Henry opened his eyes.

"Is that you, Jason?" he said, groggily putting on a show of regaining consciousness. He discovering that he didn't have to do all that much acting as he staggered to his feet.

"Yeah, it's me," Jason said, taking his arm. "C'mon, I'm going to get you home."

"I'm fine," Henry said, shaking Jason off and walking on his own.

He wobbled at first, but straightened up quickly as the determination within him grew.

Grisham, that stinking bastard, wasn't going to get away with this.

None of them were.

Chapter 7.

Alan pulled into his driveway at midnight, glad to be home at last in his own quiet Glens Falls neighborhood.

The sight of the tiny, 100-year-old house, and the knowledge that his family was safe inside, drove thoughts about Grisham lawsuits and his encounter with Charlie that morning to the back of his mind.

The house practically defined the word small, but it was comfortable enough for a family of four. Besides, Alan and his wife Alice had paid off the mortgage six months earlier. They even managed to do it a year ahead of time, thanks to the additional family income from Alice's promotion to manager at Burger King.

Alan entered the house silently, as he always did when coming home late at night. An experienced parent, he kept alert for the occasional landmine, and found one – Jimmie's fire engine, lurking at the foot of the stairs.

"How many times am I going to have to tell that kid about this?" he wondered.

The irritation drained out of him when he entered the bedroom at the top of the stairs. His seven-year-old son slept soundly, the light still on, a well-worn copy of *Mr. Popper's Penguins* open in front of him. It was the same copy Alan read many times when he was seven himself.

Alan turned out the light and put the fire engine on the bed next to Jimmie. Maybe the kid would get the hint, or maybe he'd just be happy to wake up next to it. Alan smiled at the thought either way.

Next door, Jimmie's little sister Emily slept as deeply as her brother. Alan stood for a minute, thinking about nothing at all, absorbed in simply watching his daughter breathe.

"Sleep tight," he whispered, brushing a stray lock of hair off her face.

In the master bedroom, Alan carefully secured his Glock in a gun safe, and undressed.

As usual, he tried to slip into bed without waking his wife. As usual, he failed miserably. Not that Alice ever minded. Or Alan either.

They kissed slowly, after twelve years together almost telepathically aware of each other's preferences.

"You know," Alan said in mock seriousness, "some one of these nights we're simply going to have to start getting more sleep."

"Not tonight, dear."

An unmeasured amount of time later, Alan held Alice in his arms.

He tried to empty his mind and sleep, but the day's events began rushing in to fill the space, defying Alan's efforts to contain them.

"What's wrong?" Alice said.

"Can't hide a thing from you, can I?"

Alan sighed, and risked destroying the afterglow mood by telling her about his day.

Not that Alice cared anything about Grisham. She would be incapable of taking his lawsuit seriously.

"I keep telling you," she said, when Alan reached that point in the story. "Just give me five minutes alone with that man, and your troubles would be over."

Alan grinned. "Don't tempt me."

The part about Charlie Payson, though.... Alan knew any mention of *him* was guaranteed to set off an argument.

It was bad enough that Charlie divorced Alice's best friend, Helen Winslow, years ago, and ran off with another woman.

But Brian – the late, great Brian – was Alice's brother.

On the other hand, Alan realized, Alice would kill him if she found out about any of this from someone else instead of from him. Alan squared his shoulders and took the bull by the horns.

As Alan expected, Alice stiffened noticeably when Charlie's name came up.

"If you ask me, you should have arrested the son of a bitch," Alice said, when Alan finished the story.

"No evidence. C'mon, Alice, you always want to blame him for everything," Alan said.

"And you always defend him."

"I don't defend him. He and I were best friends once, is all. I just know him better than you do."

"*Brian* was your best friend," Alice snapped. "Or have you forgotten what Charlie did to him? It hasn't even been a year!"

Alan jerked back as if she'd slapped him. He hadn't expected the fight to go this far south this fast.

He tossed back the covers, got out of bed and headed for the bathroom.

"That's over the line," he said, throwing the words back over his shoulder. "Brian was a better man than me or Charlie, and I damned well know it. You *know* I'd never forget what happened to him."

Or, Alan thought, *how Charlie got Brian killed.*

Closing the bathroom door behind him, Alan sat down on the edge of the tub.

Against his will, Alan's own private little horror movie played out yet again in his mind's eye – his midnight arrival at the industrial parking lot by the Hudson River in Glens

Falls, a few seconds too late because Charlie had deliberately misdirected him.

His two best friends from high school there. Charlie standing, Brian sprawled dead on the pavement in a spreading pool of blood from the gunshot wounds, lit up by the headlights from Alan's car.

If Alan hadn't seen the man with the gun running away, he might've blamed Charlie and killed him right then and there.

The gunman ended up dead, killed by a suspected drug dealer.

Charlie took out the gunman's boss. Alan had to give him credit for that. By luck or design, Charlie even managed to do it in legal self-defense. That part, Charlie was happy enough to tell the grand jury about.

Otherwise, Charlie gave no explanation for any of it. Alan pieced together information which suggested some sort of industrial espionage in the computer software business, but nothing definite. How drug dealers fit in was even more of a mystery.

The image of Brian, filling Alan's mind in full living color, refused to go away.

Alan felt the familiar ache rising, squeezing his chest. The pain rose inexorably, engulfing his mind, just as if he were once again at the graveside service for his grandmother, 20 years back, or for his father, a few years later. Or for Brian.

Alan went to Brian's funeral expecting he'd be better prepared. He almost succeeded in watching the pain do its harsh work as if it was happening to someone else, not him. Almost. If Alice hadn't been there, needing his strength, and giving him hers, he would have become nothing more than an oversized basket case.

Alan felt new tears coming down his face and dropping on the bathroom floor.

"Damn it, Charlie," Alan whispered. "Why the hell didn't

you trust me to go with you that night?"

And why, for that matter, did Charlie still not trust him with whatever secret was locked away in that damn genius mind of his?

Sitting in his office with Jeff Sandil the next morning, Alan yawned widely. He hadn't slept well at all. He and Alice had both apologized, once he went back to bed, but sleep wasn't much in the cards.

Jeff, occasionally wincing if he took a deep breath, insisted he was ready to go back on patrol duty. So far, the sheriff insisted on keeping him at a desk, even though Jeff's ribs were only bruised rather than broken.

After listening to Jeff griping about his inactivity, Alan started talking about his own problems. Purely in self-defense, he told himself.

Besides, Jeff was a recent immigrant, having arrived in the North Country from New York City only a year ago. If they were going to work together on this case, Jeff needed to know more about Charlie.

"So," Jeff said, "you're telling me this Payson character is a drug dealer?"

Alan had to smile, watching the way Sandil's expression changed to one of disgust. If nothing else, the deputy had the right attitude towards dealers.

"No," Alan said, losing the smile. "Charlie's no drug dealer. In fact, I pity the dealer that ever crosses paths with him. That's just the point, though."

"You think he went vigilante."

"I really don't know. Maybe."

"But you think he was involved somehow."

"I know darned well he was. At the very least, he knows more than he's saying." Alan shook his head. "Twenty-five years ago I would've said it was impossible for Charlie

Payson to commit murder. Now, I'd have to say it's only improbable."

Alan sighed, and stretched until his back made a series of small popping sounds. "I barely had enough circumstantial evidence to get Charlie in front of a grand jury last year. He proceeded to plead the Fifth with a vengeance."

Jeff nodded in commiseration. "From the way you're talking, I'm guessing the grand jury didn't indict him."

"Not even close. The DA even thanked me for wasting their time. As long as Charlie keeps his trap shut, he's got no worries."

"We'll just have to get him talking, then."

Alan couldn't help laughing out loud.

Jeff bristled, and spoke in a tone that was only half joking. "Just 'cause you're bigger than me, don't think I'll take being laughed at."

Alan stifled a final chuckle. "I'm sorry, Jeff. Really. But make Charlie Payson talk? You don't know him like I do. If there's one thing the man knows how to do, it's how to shut up."

Alan's mind drifted to the fact that he had not told the grand jury *everything* he knew about Charlie's involvement in the circumstances surrounding Brian's death.

He wondered, for the thousandth time, why in God's name he hadn't. Lingering loyalty to a one-time best friend? Some inexplicable sense that Brian wouldn't have wanted him to? Charlie's silence was somehow contagious?

Alan tried to tell himself the information wouldn't have made any difference anyway. A voice deep down inside told him that he knew this was a lie.

The sound of Jeff smacking a fist into a palm brought Alan's attention back to his office.

"Maybe we could 'encourage' the man a bit," Jeff said. The grin on his face said he was, perhaps, at least half joking.

Alan leaned forward, not joking at all. "Don't make the mistake of thinking physical intimidation will work on him. Believe it or not, he served in the Marines."

"So did I," Jeff said.

"Point taken," Alan said, "but I'm not finished. Did you know he has only one foot? The guy who ordered Brian's murder blew Charlie's left one off at the ankle with a shotgun."

Alan shook his head. "And Charlie still managed to take him out."

Jeff looked skeptical, but Alan went on. "If you see Charlie today, it's hard to tell he has any limp at all."

"So?"

"So, that means he drove himself damned hard through a crapload of physical therapy, even accounting for the high-tech prosthetic he uses."

Alan leaned back, stretched out his legs, and flexed his own two flesh-and-blood ankles. "I wouldn't be surprised if Charlie wrote the software for the prosthetic's computer brain, or at least made some custom modifications."

Jeff snorted. "It sounds like you're saying he's some kind of Renaissance man."

"Don't laugh," Alan said. "With his brains, he should have been a total computer nerd, instead of just partly, but he was too good an athlete to be allowed to go that route. On the wrestling team at Queensbury High School, he was almost as good as me, and I had 30 or 40 pounds on him."

The frown on Jeff's face told Alan the message wasn't sinking in. He considered pushing harder, but then decided it might be better to lighten the mood for the time being.

"On the other hand," he said, "Charlie does speak fluent Klingon, so that tells you something."

Jeff chuckled. "It's a relief to know something about the guy's harmless."

Alan pulled a folder out of the file cabinet next to his desk. "Here's Charlie's file, if you want to take a look."

"Sure," Jeff said, taking the folder and leafing through the pages.

"Don't misunderstand," Alan said. "Leave Charlie to me. I know you did a lot of forensic computer training with the NYPD, but with all due respect, you might be biting off more than you can chew with him."

"I might be better than you think," Jeff said.

"Actually, he might be better than *you* think. Think about that. Seriously, I'd rather see a chimpanzee with an Uzi than Charlie Payson with a laptop computer."

"That's your idea of saying something seriously?" Jeff said.

Alan sighed. "Just read the man's file, while I try to get some work done here, okay?"

Jeff nodded and began reading Charlie's file.

Alan opened another folder, the one Bill Gantry had sent him about the shooting at Henry C's. He figured he'd review it, then add his report about his interview with Charlie, for all the good it would do.

Jeff glanced up, and went back to reading Charlie's file.

Then he froze.

He looked again, staring at the crime scene photo in the report on Alan's desk. A photo of a man with a great deal of blood on the side of his head.

Jeff cleared his throat. "Uh, Alan, who the hell's that?" he said, his voice just a touch higher than he would've liked.

"Antonio Smith," Alan said. "You know, the guy who was shot in Glens Falls a couple days ago."

"Oh, yeah, of course," Jeff said.

Alan noticed the way Jeff was staring.

"You know the guy or something?" Alan asked.

"Hmm? Uh, no. Just for a second, I thought it looked like

somebody I knew in New York City, but, uh, no."

"You're sure?"

"Absolutely," Jeff said.

Jeff started to turn back to Charlie's file, then asked, "He's still alive, right?"

"Smith? At worst, a mild concussion," Alan said. "Apparently the guy's got a pretty tough skull."

"Yeah, a tough skull," Jeff mused, as if talking to himself.

He began leafing through Charlie's file again, but he was no longer reading. Thoughts about his past with the NYPD now clamored for attention in his mind.

Twenty minutes later, Alan finished going over the Henry C's report. He reached back to massage the muscles beginning to grow into tight knots at the base of his skull.

Something about the last section of the report – a transcript of the GFPD interview with Antonio Smith in the hospital – nagged at Alan's mind.

Alan would stake his reputation that Smith was hiding something.

For one thing, what was the guy doing at Henry C's an hour before opening time? Charlie said Grisham sometimes did business very early. Did that mean Smith was into something with Grisham?

Now *there* was a potential can of worms to open.

For another thing, there were Smith's own words – all very reasonable, very bland, and, if you looked at them closely, revealing nothing.

None of which necessarily implied that anything criminal was afoot, but still.

If Smith crossed his path in the future, Alan thought the man would definitely bear watching.

Windy-day whitecaps racing down the lake.

Chapter 8.

Charlie noticed that Henry Crane didn't bother to look out at the spectacular view of Lake George offered by the restaurant's lakeside windows. The guy barely picked at his food, too.

"Okay, Henry," Charlie said. "You wanted to meet for lunch, and obviously something's bugging you. Out with it."

For once, Henry got right to the point.

"Charlie, Alan McMendell called me, and wants to meet me to ask some questions about the shooting at my place," Henry said.

"So?" Charlie said.

"So, can I trust him? The cafe's hanging by a thread. I can't afford him shutting me down or anything."

"*Trust* him? Charlie said. He pondered for a few seconds.

"Sounds like you can't, if you gotta think about it," Henry said.

"Not at all," Charlie said. "I'm just trying to think of the best way to put it."

Charlie looked out the window at the whitecaps racing down the lake, and sighed glumly.

"Alan's flat-out-by-God the most trustworthy guy you'll ever meet. He's world-class straight-and-narrow. One of the two best friends I ever had, until I screwed that up."

Charlie shifted his gaze back to Henry. "Don't take him for some Dudley Do-Right, though. He's smart as hell, even by my standards."

Charlie shook his head, and sort of half smiled. "Al's been known to tell me that I'm not *quite* as smart as I think I am, but *he's* actually *smarter* than he thinks he is."

Henry halfheartedly stabbed a french fry with his fork. "So far, you're not being very encouraging," he said.

"Oh, there's more," Charlie said. "Al can be very tough-minded. If the evidence says you're guilty, he'll lock you up and throw away the key. That's actually one of the things I like about him, being a pragmatic son of a bitch myself."

Charlie chomped a massive bite out of his turkey club, and chewed until he had worn the mouthful down enough to speak again.

"Ol' Al would slip the cuffs on the president and throw the dude's ass in jail if the evidence said he was guilty."

Henry grinned, his downer attitude starting to lift. "Are you saying that because he's thrown *your* ass in jail?"

Charlie laughed, losing his own downer attitude.

"Yeah, my old semi-buddy did do that, didn't he? And he just might do it again someday, for all I know. What can I say? He may be smart and tough-minded, but he's not immune to making mistakes."

"Of course, Charlie," Henry said. "You're the only one around here who never makes mistakes."

Charlie paused before attacking his sandwich again. "If only, Henry. Man, if only."

Chapter 9.

Jeff sat at his computer terminal at the Sheriff's Department. A bit more composed now, he decided to put his Smith problem on hold and take on the problem he could deal with directly.

So, this Charlie Payson character thought he was a big deal with computers?

We'll see about that, Jeff thought. Alan didn't need to know about this either, for now.

Jeff had been fooling around with computers ever since he was five years old. He'd even gained some reputation as a hacker before hearing the call of law enforcement.

Since then, he'd taken every computer crime course available through the NYPD. He'd participated on the team that busted some of the most skilled computer criminals in the city. He had even contrived some unauthorized "seminars" to learn what he could from those very same perps.

It didn't seem likely that Payson was on their level. This Lake George-Glens Falls area was great, but New York City it was not. And, even if Payson was that good, unlikely though that might be, nobody's invulnerable.

Jeff mapped out an approach in his mind, and got to work.

Some time later, he pushed himself away from his keyboard and shook his head ruefully.

"Okay, I'll give you round one," he muttered.

It hadn't taken Jeff long to locate Payson's computer system on the Internet. The system, although elegant, manifested some of the most arcane architecture Jeff had ever seen. He'd been butting his head against its firewalls without a hint of getting anywhere.

So, the guy was better than expected, probably an obsessive-compulsive nut about security. On the other hand, that might be a weakness in itself.

Jeff made a call to his old NYPD computer crime team leader. A short time later, an email arrived describing the latest security approaches an obsessive-compulsive security nut would be likely to use, along with some suggestions on how to crack them.

Newly armed, Jeff went to work.

In a mere five minutes, he was in, and the supposedly hot shit Payson didn't know a thing about it.

Charlie frowned at his computer screen, the lines in his forehead growing deeper and deeper.

"Man, I leave you guys alone for a couple hours, and look what happens," he said to the laptop array in his Lake George office.

Someone, some *unauthorized personnel,* was attempting to enter his computer system.

Somebody *good.* Charlie stared as the son of a bitch abruptly slipped through the stage-one firewall.

"Yeah, real good," Charlie muttered, but for the moment, he waived the intruder's skill away as a secondary concern.

The *real concern* was that anybody was looking at all.

Somewhere, somehow, Charlie had attracted somebody's attention.

That was the real problem.

Charlie knew quite well that the best way to hide was to not have anybody looking for you in the first place. He generally tried to avoid activity that might draw attention, and had dedicated many an hour of computer time to hiding all traces when said activity was unavoidable.

He sighed heavily. Having someone looking was a problem that might have to be dealt with harshly.

Charlie recalled his Marine Corps days, and a certain operation down in Central America.

Officially, no such thing had ever occurred, of course, but Charlie and his squad had "dealt harshly" with...well, how many rebels was it? Charlie hadn't bothered to count.

And, more recently, there was Adam Hartwicke, the bastard responsible for Brian's death. Charlie generally favored making it quick, if there was no way to avoid taking things to the harshest extreme, but Hartwicke, yeah, *that* sorry excuse for a human being should have taken a lot longer.

Charlie turned his attention back to his computer screen. At least his stage two defense system was working as designed. It had shunted the intruder into a dummy virtual hard drive, full of apparently interesting files and folders which were in reality totally useless.

Typing at furious speed, Charlie quickly called up a subroutine to backtrack the intruder.

Considering his own clandestine computer activities, Charlie knew he shouldn't complain if someone did likewise to him.

Nevertheless, actions have consequences. Charlie was well aware that he had managed to outrun his own consequences for quite a while now. In the meantime, he could see to it that the intruder's consequences caught up, big-time.

"Jumping crap," Charlie muttered, when the backtracker finished its work.

He'd expected maybe someone federal, or perhaps some amateur hired by Grisham. Instead, the intruder's computer resided in the freakin' County Sheriff's Department offices.

Alan? No, his old semi-friend was smart. In fact, considerably smarter than the big lug gave himself credit for. However, Charlie knew for a fact that Alan didn't have the computer skills.

Charlie checked to make sure the intruder was still stuck in stage two. Then he employed the backdoor access he had Trojan Horsed into the Sheriff Department computers years earlier.

He called up the department payroll and scrolled through the names. One name practically leapt off the screen.

Jeff Sandil.

Yeah, Charlie remember that name from ten years or so back. Promising young hacker who suddenly disappeared, never to be heard from again.

Until now.

"Man, you'll wish you'd stayed disappeared by the time I get done with you," Charlie said.

He got Sandil's address from the department database. The place wasn't far, just a couple miles away in one of the more sparsely settled sections of Lake George.

Charlie smiled grimly. An *informal* location, sparsely settled, would definitely be better for this encounter than the Sheriff's Department offices.

Charlie monitored Sandil's activities, curious to see what the dude had by way of style.

Charlie watched calmly for a minute, then jerked forward. Out of nowhere, the "dude" suddenly cleared the dummy files.

Even as Charlie pushed his typing speed to the max, trying to steer the deputy away, he realized what had happened.

Sandil was friggin' good indeed. The guy had a subroutine of his own running, one of those auto-hacking jobs that poked around looking for access on its own while Sandil was ostensibly checking out data files.

Charlie kicked himself for not taking the situation more seriously.

If you let your guard down, it doesn't matter that you're more skilled than your opponent.

Complacency, he thought. *It'll kill you. Or kill* somebody, *anyway.*

With Sandil some small number of nanoseconds away from violating Charlie's real system, Charlie abruptly stopped typing and pulled the high-speed DSL cable out of his laptop network's communications router.

"Suck on that," Charlie said.

Then he spent the next hour tracking down and eradicating the auto-hacker and making triple and quadruple sure his system was clean. He knew how hard it was to eradicate *his own* viruses, worms, Trojan Horses, etc., and he wasn't going to take any chances with someone else's.

Especially with someone this good.

Yeah, Sandil was way too good.

Way too good to take any chances with at all, Charlie realized.

He set to work doing a full scale purge of all sensitive data and programs in his real system.

Not that Charlie believed anything short of an NSA supercomputer could have gotten into the *really* good stuff in less than a decade or so, but on the other hand, Sandil shouldn't have gotten nearly as far as he did.

Charlie also believed that no amount of firewalls, encryptions, passwords, eccentric system structure, or abstruse methods of hiding files can ever give you an absolute, 100 percent guarantee. After all, look at all the systems he himself was able to get into.

By the time Charlie finished the purge, not even the NSA could retrieve the really good stuff, because it just wasn't there.

It was all duplicated on Charlie's backup array of computers at a different location, of course. And to think, he had almost not installed the hidden backup array on the basis that going to that much trouble seemed just a little *too* paranoid.

Speaking of paranoia, Charlie thought, he wondered if the purge would be enough. Maybe. Maybe not.

In all honesty, Charlie had to admit that didn't know whether he had pulled the plug soon enough. Sandil might've gotten a glimpse of things he never should've seen.

Any glimpse at all would have made a guy like Sandil overwhelmingly curious, and as long as he kept on looking, he was still a threat.

It occurred to Charlie that, as long as a more paranoid approach seemed to be the appropriate order of the day, he ought to have another talk with Grisham. It was just possible that the information Grisham had tried to blackmail him with could be more damaging than Charlie initially thought.

Charlie made sure he had Sandil's address memorized.

Grisham's address, he already knew.

Chapter 10.

Jeff entered the main entrance of the hospital for his scheduled check up on the progress of his injuries.

His chest and arm still ached considerably, but they were coming around.

What he was really smarting from, though, was his failure to reenter Payson's computer system.

Just when Jeff finally caught a glimpse of the good stuff, Payson had somehow shut him out. Jeff's attempts to reenter had gone nowhere.

It was as if Payson had gone offline completely, or turned his computer off or something. Well, maybe he had. That would be kind of a low-tech defense for someone of Payson's caliber, but effective.

Jeff hadn't seen much of the geek's inner system, but the glimpse was enough, almost against his will, to reawaken Jeff's old hacking instincts.

And maybe even scare him a little, too. McMendell was right about Payson's brilliance, and the geek was into some damn radical shit, no doubt about it.

An auto-hacking program had gotten him into Payson's system. What Payson had, if Jeff could believe what he had briefly seen, was like that auto-hacker on about 10,000 pounds of steroids.

Not that it was complex. Quite the opposite. The approach was simplicity itself. Elegant. As close to undetectable as you could get.

And powerful.

With something like that at his disposal, Payson might have back door access to damn near every computer in the country.

The more Jeff thought about it, the more he became convinced of the need to know just what the hell Payson was up to.

He'd tell Al about this, and about Smith too, when they met first thing tomorrow.

Lost in thought, Jeff failed to notice the large gentleman in a wheelchair being wheeled to the hospital exit.

Smith, screening his face by holding a hand up to the bandage on his head, watched through the slits between his fingers as the deputy passed.

Jeff Sandil? he thought. *Is this where the hell he went when he disappeared from Brooklyn?*

This certainly put a new wrinkle on every damn thing. This could blow the whole deal, is what it could do.

Smith stood when the wheelchair reached the exit, and walked briskly to the taxi waiting for him.

Sandil, Smith thought. What the crap was he doing here, in a Sheriff's Department uniform, no less?

This made it necessary to track down a whole new line of information.

Lucky for Smith, he knew right where to start inquiring.

Thoughts of investigating anyone, Charlie Payson or otherwise, left Jeff Sandil's mind as he turned off the paved road. He eased his Chevy S-10 pickup truck down the quarter-mile gravel driveway to his small, two-bedroom ranch style house.

As he got of the truck, a red squirrel chattered at him from the white pine trees surrounding the yard. At least, they looked like the white pines in the tree book Jeff had borrowed from Crandall Library.

Jeff shook his head, and grinned. Here he was, New York City born and raised, a fifth-generation Brooklyn kid, living in a house where his nearest neighbor was a quarter mile away, driving a pickup truck, and learning to recognize trees.

He'd wanted to get away from the city, get himself out from under that place once and for all. He'd come a damn long way.

His grin faded. The image he'd seen in the report on "Antonio Smith" reared its ugly head in his mind.

Maybe, Jeff thought, he hadn't come far enough.

Maybe he should call Al about Smith, and about Payson too, right now.

Al was his partner, and was fast becoming his friend. He owed him that much.

The voice startled him. "We need, as they say, to talk."

Jeff spun around, ready to draw his pistol on the man standing behind him. Jeff hadn't heard a sound from the guy's approach, a hell of a trick on loose gravel.

The guy raised a hand in a placating gesture. "Easy, Sandil. I said I wanted to talk, not get shot."

"What the hell are you doing here?" Jeff said. "And how did you find out where I live? Everything about this place is unlisted."

The intruder shrugged. "What can I say? I'm good with information. I take it you're surprised to see me."

"Not really," Jeff said. "I had a feeling I was going to have to deal with you sooner or later."

The guy smiled, slowly. "Think you're ready to deal with me?"

Jeff didn't smile back. "I think I know what makes you tick."

"Is that right? You tell McMendell about it?"

"Maybe. Maybe not."

"In other words, no." The guy shook his head, almost sadly. "Maybe you should have."

Jeff saw the gun, materialized as if by magic.

He saw the flash, felt the bullet crash into his forehead. He staggered.

His arm moved feebly, as if he was thinking about trying to pull his own gun. His arm seemed to lose interest about halfway there. He dropped, landing face down on the unyielding gravel.

The kick in his ribs rolled him over, face up.

He saw blue sky framed by trees, and a face. He heard a voice saying something he vaguely thought he should be interested in.

"How 'bout that. You *do* look surprised, after all. Whatta ya think? Am I going to surprise Grisham, too?

Jeff lay on his back, unmoving. Confusing images rambled through his damaged brain as random synapses fired.

Another face appeared in his line of vision. A nice face. A feeling of accomplishment surged through him as the face suddenly matched to a name.

Karen. His...neighbor. Yes, that was the word.

An idea began to grow. Something Jeff should do.

Something important.

But so many distracting thoughts swirled, competing for his attention. The idea began to fade.

He happened to notice that the face...Karen, yes...was holding a...a cell phone.

That was the idea. Talking.

More synapses fired, perhaps not quite so randomly.

"He's good with information," Jeff said. Calmly, with only a bit of slurring, as if he had downed four beers but not the whole sixpack.

It seemed that maybe there should be something more, some other important words, but then the idea truly faded.

All the confusing images faded away too, and there was finally peace and quiet.

Three-quarter moon over the Grisham mansion on Lake George

Chapter 11.

Alan drove through the gateway to the Grisham mansion, one of the survivors of the old "Millionaire's Row" of mansions built along the west shore of Lake George a century earlier, more or less, between the Village of Lake George to the south and the hamlet of Bolton Landing to the north.

Boulders of native granite from the Adirondack Mountains formed the gate pillars, looming massive in the pale light of a three-quarter moon.

The driveway wound through sculpted lawns and perfectly spaced blue spruce trees to the imposing main house, likewise made of native Adirondack stone.

Wet shoreline smells from the lake drifted on the night

air, mixing with the fading bouquet of a lawn that must have been freshly mowed that afternoon.

Alan found dozens of cars parked along edges of the driveway and clustered on the lawn around the front door.

Just great. Right when Alan wanted to interrogate Grisham in private, the son of a bitch was throwing one of his parties.

A primer-black '72 Chevy Nova SS with a turbocharger sticking out of the hood pulled in behind Alan. Definitely out of place among the BMW's, Porches, SUV's and such of the crowd Grisham ran with.

Alan recognized the Nova instantly. It belonged to Charlie Payson.

Alan groaned, but admitted to himself that he felt a certain sense of inevitability to Charlie's arrival.

Back in their high school days, Charlie, Brian, and Alan had always shown up, strictly uninvited, whenever Grisham threw a party.

Surprisingly enough, Grisham never tossed them out. Of course, back then they were only teenagers screwing around.

Alan took a deep breath. He hauled his mind back to the present, resenting the distraction. His partner had been wounded. Jeff might even be dead. And God help Grisham if he was involved.

Or Charlie if he got in the way, for that matter.

Alan got out of his car. He took a few quick steps and blocked Charlie's door from opening.

"Charlie. What the hell are you doing here?"

Charlie grinned, as if their argument the day before had never happened.

"What else? I'm crashing the party," he said. He looked Alan up and down. "Same as you, I'm guessing."

"I don't have time for this crap," Alan said. "Jeff Sandil's been shot."

Charlie gaped at him, looking for all the world as if he were genuinely surprised. "You're kidding. When?"

"About 30 minutes ago. He was shot. In the head."

Charlie's expression didn't change, but Alan could tell his one-time friend's brain was kicking into high gear.

"Damn!" Charlie said. "You suspect the Grishams, of course."

"It doesn't take any genius to figure that out," Alan said.

"Al, old buddy, it also doesn't take any freakin' genius to see you're here without a partner, and you're going off half-cocked. You need me to watch your back."

"I need someone," Alan conceded. "God help me if it's you."

"Good. It's a done deal then," Charlie said. He grinned knowingly. "Besides, this way you can keep an eye on *me,* too."

Alan rolled his eyes, but took a step back, allowing Charlie out of his car.

"Okay, Charlie. Just don't slow me down."

"Against Grisham? I wouldn't dream of it."

They walked to the mansion's main entryway.

"How'd you know Grisham was throwing a party?" Alan asked.

Charlie shrugged. "You know how good I am with information."

They stepped up to the door.

"I'm not going off half-cocked," Alan said.

Charlie nodded. "Not with me here to talk some sense into you."

"Don't push it, Chuck."

"Don't call me that," Charlie said.

He opened the door without bothering to knock, and they entered the mansion.

They found a good-sized crowd of people in the ornate

main hall, but Charlie thought it wasn't as packed as they'd seen at some Grisham parties.

Henry Crane walked by. He was wearing a white apron over a white shirt and black bow tie, and hefted a large tray of hors d'oeuvres.

"Henry?" Charlie said. "What the hell are you doing here?"

"Catering, what the hell's it look like?" Henry said, with uncharacteristic belligerence, although his eyes shifted nervously.

Charlie glanced at Alan, who was working his way on through the crowd.

Charlie turned back to Henry. "You're still working for Grisham, after what you told me happened at the casino?"

"I...hey, you're still working for him," Henry said.

"Yeah, well...okay, touché, man," Charlie said. "But still."

"Besides," Henry said. "Working here presents certain opportunities, you know, for..." Henry's voice dropped down to a whisper. "...Revenge."

Charlie grinned. "Fair enough. But listen, don't go anything drastic until I talk to you first, okay?"

Henry shifted his tray to a more comfortable position.

"You're trying to be a friend, but you're not the boss of me, Charlie. I've got a right to do this the way I want."

"Maybe so, but don't make me have to bail you out of jail."

Henry flared suddenly.

"I'm not *making* you do anything. Maybe you should butt out. I don't need you to babysit me."

Henry stalked off, leaving Charlie standing without even a chance to snag an hors d'oeuvre from the tray.

Charlie started to follow, but then spotted Alan scanning the crowd for Grisham.

Charlie cursed. Something in Henry's attitude unsettled him, but he knew Alan had to be the priority at the moment.

A thought occurred to Charlie as he caught up to Alan. It

seemed unlikely, but on the other hand he'd never seen Henry in this kind of a mood before. There was no telling what an incensed caterer might do.

"Don't eat any of the food, man," Charlie told Alan.

"What?" Alan said. "I'm not hungry."

"That's a first. But good. That makes my job of watching your back that much easier."

Alan appeared to ignore the comment. He pointed across the room. "There's Alfred. He'll know where Grisham is."

Charlie suppressed a grin. The Grisham family butler, John Alfred, never failed to remind Charlie of Alfred, Batman's butler in the comic books.

Alfred had been old 20-some years ago, at least in Charlie's teenager eyes. There was no telling how old he was now, but he still stood as stiffly erect as ever.

"Detective McMendell," Alfred said as they approached. He raised an eyebrow at Charlie. "Master Charles."

"Alfredo," Charlie said. "The lord of the manor about, by any chance?" He managed to restrain the old teenager urge to ask for Bruce Wayne.

Alfred ignored Charlie, and looked at Alan, who nodded.

Alfred went to a wall-mounted intercom, and spoke briefly.

Then he addressed Alan. "This way, sir."

The butler led them to the open central staircase leading to the second floor.

Charlie spotted Mr. Smith heading for the stairs, then quickly turn aside when Alan came into view.

Interesting, Charlie thought. As far as he knew, Alan and Smith had never met, and Alan was in civilian clothes. Smith obviously tagged Alan as a cop anyway, and just as obviously wanted to avoid him.

Charlie filed that away as one more piece of information to add to his growing body of data on "Antonio Smith."

Alfred led the way to the mansion's second-floor library, where Grisham sat in a steel and chrome chair, some sort of artsy designer contraption, behind a matching steel and chrome desk.

Charlie assumed the discord between the furniture and the library's antique cherry bookshelves and darkly stained oak-paneled walls was meant to impress upon visitors just how damned expensive such items must be.

Grisham didn't bother to get up when Alfred ushered Alan and Charlie into the room.

"Well, well. McMendell and Payson, crashing the party," Grisham said, unsmiling. "Just like old times."

"Enough of this crap," Alan said. "My partner's been shot. He's probably dead."

"What?" Grisham said.

Even as carefully as Alan was watching, he couldn't tell if Grisham was genuinely shocked, or just giving an excellent imitation.

Alan stepped around the desk and moved in close, forcing Grisham to crane his neck to maintain eye contact.

"Deputy Jeff Sandal was shot this evening," Alan said. "Where was your son about 40 minutes ago? Where were *you,* for that matter?"

Grisham leaned back in his chair, easing the angle of his neck, and folded his arms. His eyes remained locked on Alan's.

"We've been here all day," Grisham said. "You'll find dozens of witnesses. Ask around."

"I will," Alan said.

"Although," Grisham said, "if you want to do it on my property, you'll have to wait until my lawyer gets here first. He might even want you to get a warrant."

Grisham raised a hand in a mock magnanimous gesture. "In the meantime, feel free to wait outside on the lawn."

Alan growled, then abruptly spun around and left the room, dragging Charlie by the arm.

"What the hell?" Charlie said, at the bottom of the stairs. "You mean you're actually leaving?"

"My hands are tied. This has to be done absolutely legally."

"Yeah? Well, you'd be the expert on that."

Charlie wrenched his arm loose from Alan's grip, and started back up the steps towards Grisham's office.

"What are you doing? We have to leave the dickhead alone," Alan said. "At least for now."

"*We* don't have to do anything," Charlie said. "Grisham kicked *you* out. He didn't say anything to me. I, in fact, have another matter entirely to discuss with him."

Alan looked disgusted. "So, you really are consorting with the enemy. Listen, my friend. If you do *anything* to screw up this investigation...."

"Farthest thing from my mind."

Alan's look of disgust changed to one of outright pain. "Yeah, right," he said. "Look, just do me a favor, and keep your nose out of this."

"To the maximum extent possible."

"To the *full* extent," Alan said. "Trust me, you *do not* want to cross me on this."

Charlie nodded. "Okay, already. Message received."

He turned back toward the stairs, then looked back, an uncharacteristically sheepish expression on his face. "I'm sorry, man, but this thing with Grisham was in play before your partner got shot. It's something I just can't leave hanging."

Alan shook his head, and headed for the front door. As he did, he recognized Smith, the big guy from the Henry C's shooting, watching Charlie climb the stairs.

It occurred to him to wonder what Smith was doing at

Grisham's party, but there was too much else on his mind for him to give it much thought.

Alan stepped outside and let the cool night air wash over him, with its lakeside humidity and scent of mowed lawn.

Leaning against his car, he breathed deeply, trying to calm his mind.

After a couple minutes, his worry and grief about Jeff remained, but some order had returned to his disjointed thoughts.

So, Grisham wanted a warrant, did he? Alan flipped open his cellphone to call the DA to start the process.

The three gunshot blasts from inside the house stopped him.

Chapter 12.

Gunshots? In the house, maybe upstairs? Sounded like, Alan thought.

Three more bangs.

Gunshots! Definitely.

Drawing his Glock .40 S&W, Alan reached Grisham's front door in seconds and wrenched it open.

He was halfway to the stairs, using his imposing size to shove his way through the confused party crowd, when a seventh shot sounded.

A lighter caliber this time. Maybe a .22.

Definitely upstairs.

Alan took the stairs three at a time.

He slowed at the top, reminding himself that he wore no bulletproof vest.

And he had no backup, unless he counted Charlie, which he didn't. Charlie was nowhere to be seen anyway.

Alan carefully checked out the hallway to Grisham's office. No one in sight.

He quickly worked his way to the office.

He didn't know anyone, including himself, who possessed any sympathy for Carl Grisham, but Alan cursed softly when he found the body.

Kenny raced into his bedroom in the Grisham mansion. He paced rapidly back and forth across the 40-foot expanse of the room.

The room had been his for as long as he could remember. His grandparents, while they were still alive, told him that the room had originally been his father's, when his father was a child.

Now his father was dead.

The bloody images careening through Kenny's mind left no doubt of that.

His pacing led him to the room's stone fireplace.

At long last, his father was dead.

It was time for a celebration.

Kenny bent over and reached up into the chimney. His sweaty fingers scrabbled over the hidden shelf inside the flue, searching for the vial and the pipe. After a frantic few seconds, his fingers found their goal, and closed eagerly on the prize.

Kenny hauled his small treasures out into the light. He wiped in disgust at the soot and cobwebs adorning his hand, but even that couldn't dim his mood.

His father was dead, at long last.

Kenny opened the vial in haste, fumbling with the lid. He ordered himself to slow down.

His father was dead. The proper solemnity was required.

Kenny laughed, a small, brief cackle. Yes, solemnity by all means.

He expertly dumped a piece of crack from the vial into the pipe. He fished his lighter out of his pants pocket, and flicked on the flame.

He was shaking with anticipation now, which made the knock on the door all the more annoying.

He flicked off the lighter, and yelled, "What?"

"I'm sorry to disturb you, sir," came John Alfred's voice from the other side of the door. Funny, the butler had always called him "Master Kenneth" before, instead of "sir."

"What is it, Alfred?" Kenny said. He usually found it quite amusing to call him that, as if he was talking to Batman's butler. The humor escaped him at the moment.

"Sir, the guests are quite upset. Someone needs to talk to them."

"What're ya telling me for?"

"Well, sir, you are the head of the house now."

Kenny considered this for a moment. "Yeah, whatever. I'll be there in ten minutes."

"Forgive me, sir, but I don't believe that Investigator McMendell will want to wait that long. He wants to talk to you as well."

Alan McMendell. Now there was a real mood dimmer.

"Screw what he wants," Kenny said. "Tell him I'll be there when I'm ready."

"Very good, sir. Oh, by the way, I've taken the liberty of calling your father's lawyer. That is, your lawyer, sir."

Kenny hesitated. "Thank you," he said eventually. Another hesitation, then, "You're a good man, Alfred."

"Thank you, sir."

Was it Kenny's imagination, or did Alfred sound faintly surprised at the compliment?

When Kenny was sure the butler was gone, he re-flicked his lighter. Guests. Police investigators. Butlers.

Didn't they know his father was dead? It was time to celebrate.

He brought the flame close to the crystalized cocaine. His heart was beating faster already.

Butlers. Guests. What the hell did they know?

His father was gone. He *wanted* this celebration. But the flame remained inches away from the crack.

"C'mon," he said. "Dad's gone. You know you want this."

His body *needed* it, Kenny was all too aware. He could feel the craving, like an insistent animal raging on his....

Kenny almost smiled. Yes, exactly like a damned monkey on his back, just like that public service commercial he'd seen on TV years ago. Monkey? Damned gorilla, more like.

To hell with what his body *needed,* Kenny told himself. He *wanted* this. For himself. To celebrate, of course.

The old man was dead. No more interference, no more making Kenny's life miserable, no more beat downs.

Now, as Alfred pointed out, Kenny was the head of House Grisham. God, that felt good to hear.

And yet, he wasn't celebrating, not the way he would be if he would just touch the stupid flame to this stupid piece of rock.

From out of nowhere, he remembered that bastard McMendell saying, "You do have a freaking brain, or you did before you discovered drugs, anyway."

"Fuck you," Kenny said.

From way out of nowhere, his father's voice came into his mind. "Stop being a wimp. You're the head of the house now, son."

"Shut up," Kenny said, to the voice he just then realized he was never going to hear again.

The craving in Kenny's body sensed its opportunity. His hand began moving the flame inexorably closer, until it was almost caressing the little crystal.

"You do have a freaking brain," McMendell's voice reminded in Kenny's head again. Kenny ignored it, and watched the flame edge another hundredth of an inch closer.

"Head of the house now." Alfred's voice in his head. Alfred's. Not his father's.

The bloody image of Kenny's last sight of his father surged, filling Kenny's mind. He was never going to hear his father's voice again.

Kenny's hands started shaking. The lighter flame, and the pipe with its sweet little load of release, began blurring from the water gathering in his eyes.

It would be so easy, to breath in those crack fumes. To celebrate, to forget, to lose himself, to....He shut his eyes tightly....To make the pain go away.

His father was dead.

Kenny choked back one sob, two, then gave up and wept uncontrollably.

A minute or so later, his father's voice came to him one last time.

"Enough already. Is this the way the head of the Grisham family acts?"

"No, Dad."

Kenny looked at the flame still burning in his hand, felt the unabated pull of the pipe and its small cargo.

The decision, who he was and what he would be, still needed to be made.

Kenny stopped and actually looked at himself, for what certainly felt like the first time in his life.

One sweaty young kid, with an easy way out waiting right there in his hands.

The head of House Grisham, with a freaking brain addicted to a highly dangerous cocaine derivative.

"Fuck," Kenny muttered, grinding his teeth.

Then he straightened his shoulders and slowly, deliberately, for once in his life very carefully, put every ounce of will he possessed into making a decision.

Chapter 13.

Alan examined Grisham's body.

A head shot.

Just like Jeff.

Just like Smith, too.

No, that wasn't quite right.

Jeff and Grisham took it right in the middle of the forehead. Mr. Smith was shot from the side.

Which was suggestive, but without more information, didn't really mean squat.

Alan looked up as Charlie came in.

"Well," Charlie said, "if you start with his enemies, that narrows it down to about half the county."

"Charlie, I'd appreciate it if you'd shut up," Alan said. "You shouldn't be in here anyway. You're contaminating my crime scene."

Charlie ignored him. "Yeesh! Look at all this blood!"

Alan took note that "all this blood" didn't really seem to be upsetting Charlie in the slightest.

Charlie went on, "A head shot apparently did him in, but what's up with this abdomen wound? A knife, you think?"

Charlie pointed to a gash running down Grisham's chest, from which large amounts of blood had soaked Grisham's shirt, his leather chair, and the hardwood floor beneath it.

The small hole in Grisham's forehead, by contrast, had produced hardly any blood.

"I was wondering about that myself," Alan said. "And I mean it. Shut up and get out, but don't leave the house. I'm going to want to interview you."

"Interview *me?* What am I? A suspect?"

Alan eyed him speculatively. "You're smart enough to know I have to interview everybody in the house. Why would you jump to conclusions about being a suspect?"

Charlie ignored the question. He pointed to the Colt on the desk. "That's obviously Grisham's gun, and I heard six heavy-caliber shots fired."

He looked at the walls, frowned, then looked up at the ceiling.

"Six bullet holes in the walls and ceiling, and no sign of anyone else's blood," Charlie went on. "Grisham put up quite a fight. You can't say much for his marksmanship, though."

Alan muttered a curse under his breath. Charlie's observations and conclusions matched his own.

Kenny took one last, longing look at the crack pipe in his hands. Then before he could change his mind, he threw the pipe and the vial of crack into his bedroom fireplace. He turned on the gas burner, and lit the propane with the lighter.

The gas took off with a whoosh, lightly singing the hairs on the back of Kenny's hand.

He watched the little pieces of crack snapping and popping as their fumes went harmlessly up the chimney. His body craved those fumes. Kenny let them go anyway.

"Maybe the head of the damned House Grisham does have a freakin' brain after all," Kenny said.

His freakin' brain imagined Investigator McMendell's voice adding, "You're going to need it."

Kenny opened the door to his closet. The insanely well-tailored, dark blue Epczkha business suit waited, unworn except for the day his father had forced him to try it on so the tailor could make those anal-retentive adjustments.

Kenny noticed he was thinking about his father now without seeing blood everywhere.

Kenny slipped into the suit, as if putting on a second skin. He admired his appearance in the full-length mirror on the wall next to the closet door. He recalled the photograph of his father in the library, as a young man just graduated from Harvard.

If I gave myself a shave, Kenny thought, *I could* be *my father.* It took only a minute with his electric razor. He'd probably want a haircut too, but he'd have to arrange that later.

Kenny then searched his CD collection for something to put on the house-wide sound system. Something for his guests. Something suitable to the occasion.

He found rap, heavy metal, a classic Derek and the Dominos his father had given him on a long-ago Christmas.

His father was dead, dead and gone. Nothing in the collection, not even his father's gift, seemed right to the new head of House Grisham.

He keyed the house's wireless intercom to Alfred's security code. Alfred answered immediately, and Kenny gave the butler instructions.

The adamantly soft rock that had been playing on the house stereo system abruptly quit with a loud electronic *click,* interrupting Alan's train of thought.

New music came on almost immediately.

Alan welcomed the change – a solo electric guitar, playing the Blues. Alan tried and failed to recognize the artist, in spite of the extensive collection of Blues recordings he and Alice owned.

Alan listened intently. Whoever the performer was, he, or she, was doing a darned good job of mixing the fresh power and energy of life with the grief of loss.

"Nice stuff. B.B. King, maybe," Charlie said. "Damned appropriate for the occasion."

"Shut up," Alan said.

John Alfred appeared at his right shoulder.

"Mr. Grisham will see you now, Investigator McMendell," the butler said.

"Mr. Grisham?" Alan nodded toward the body on the floor. "Mr. Grisham's dead."

"Mr. *Kenneth* Grisham," Alfred said. His tone suggested that only an idiot wouldn't have known that.

"You workin' for him now, Alfie?" Charlie said, before Alan could tell him to shut up again. "You know he might have killed your boss."

"Kenneth *is* my boss now," Alfred said. "And for all I know, Master Charles, *you* might have killed his father."

Charlie made no reply to that.

"Thank you, Alfred," Alan said. "I've been trying to shut Charlie up all evening."

"My pleasure, sir." Alfred's face remained as impassive as ever, but Alan thought he saw a twinkle in the old man's eyes.

"Well," Alan said, "let's go see young Mr. Grisham."

When Charlie started to come with them, Alan put out an arm like an offensive lineman about to clothesline a linebacker.

"*You* can stay here, Master Charles," Alan said. "Or rather, you can go downstairs and wait with everybody else."

Charlie looked wounded for a second, then shrugged. "I guess I should at least be glad Alfred didn't call me Chuck."

Henry flushed the toilet in the servants' quarters bathroom. The material he had just puked up swirled down the drain into the never-never land of the Grisham mansion septic system.

Henry had kept his limited supply of cool during the heat of the moment. In the post-adrenaline let down, though, his guts had reacted very badly indeed.

Henry didn't blame his guts. Not at all.

All that blood.

Yes, it was only Grisham's blood, and the SOB deserved whatever happened to him. But still.

So *much* blood.

"Get it together, Henry," Henry said to himself. He reminded himself that Grisham might've gotten what he deserved, but the *casino* was still there to be dealt with.

And *Frank Banfield* still needed to get his.

The kid, Jason....

Henry cursed. Thinking about Jason was taking the edge off his righteous anger.

Yeah, Jason was part of the casino, had looked Henry in the eye and cheated him – but the kid was still only a kid.

"Damn punk," Henry said. But he resolved to figure some way to get Jason out of the line of fire for what was to come.

Chapter 14.

Alfred led Alan down a hallway to the mansion's library.

As Alan followed, something about the guitar work playing on the sound system nagged at him.

He knew Charlie was wrong about the artist. It wasn't B.B. King. The style was similar, but Alan heard a subtle difference, something under the surface.

That was it. The undertone.

Angry.

Pissed off.

In-your-face.

A *punk kid* undertone.

"Oh, man, don't tell me...." Alan muttered.

Alfred opened the library door, confirming Alan's sudden intuition.

Kenny sat on the edge of a desk at one end of the room, his hands moving with easy authority over the electric guitar hanging from the strap around his neck.

Lost in the music, Kenny ignored everything around him. He kept on playing.

Alan glanced at Alfred, who instantly took the hint and left, closing the door behind him.

Alan didn't interrupt Kenny. The kid's father had just died, after all. That deserved at least a little respect.

Assuming, of course, that the kid hadn't committed patricide.

Alan used the time to study Kenny.

Forget the music. The business suit was the real shocker.

The resemblance it gave Kenny to a young Carl Grisham was uncanny. For a moment Alan imagined himself back in the halls of Queensbury High School, expecting yet another disparaging dig from Carl about "big dumb jocks."

Alan held his position until Kenny finished playing, a solid five minutes later.

"Didn't know you played," Alan said. "I'm impressed."

Kenny looked up. "Guess you could say I've got motivation tonight."

Alan noticed Kenny's eyes – bloodshot, to be sure, but possessing neither a manic touch nor a glassy emptiness. For a wonder, especially under the circumstances, the kid was actually sober.

"My condolences about your father," Alan said.

"Thanks, dude." Kenny set aside the guitar. His hands began shaking.

Sober? Yes. Going through withdrawal? Likely.

"You're being very polite," Kenny said. "It's okay. You can ask what you need to ask."

Alan considered the statement, and the fact that Kenny was sober. Was it actually possible the kid was starting to grow up?

Then Alan remembered Jeff. Kenny shot him once. Maybe again, to finish the job.

"I don't need your permission," Alan said abruptly. Then another thought occurred to him. This had to be by the book.

"You know you can have a lawyer present, don't you?" he asked.

Kenny nodded calmly. "I already know what my father's lawyer would tell me – keep my mouth shut."

"So, for the record, you're waiving your right to a lawyer?"

"For the time being."

"Okay then." Alan looked Kenny directly in the bloodshot eyes. "Did you put a bullet in Jeff Sandil's forehead earlier today?"

"What? I thought you were going to ask if I...my father..."

Kenny's voice trailed off, then, "Sandil's been *shot*? Just like my father?"

Alan watched him carefully, and sighed inwardly. He'd interviewed Kenny enough times in the past to know when the kid was putting on an act.

"Yeah," Alan said. "Jeff's not dead yet, but it doesn't look good."

"I'm...sorry, dude," Kenny said.

"Yeah, that's real big of you, considering that you did try to kill him before."

Kenny said nothing.

Alan almost began to doubt his own perceptions – the kid looked embarrassed, maybe even ashamed.

"Wait a minute," Alan said. "You said Jeff was shot just like your father. How do you know how your father was shot? *Did you shoot him?*"

Kenny straightened up in his chair. "No. Of course not." He sort of half smiled. "I might have felt like killing the old bastard occasionally, but not really. He was my *father,* dude."

Alan sighed again, outwardly this time. Kenny was telling the truth, as far as Alan could tell.

"So, you saw the, uh, body?" Alan said.

Kenny nodded. "I heard shots, from the other end of the house. I didn't know what the hell the old man was up to, and frankly I didn't care."

You were going through withdrawal, Alan thought, but he kept silent, letting Kenny tell the story.

"Then I heard the last shot," Kenny went on. "It sounded different. For some reason, that made me curious. I came in the back door to the office. I saw him, saw all the blood, and I knew he was dead. Then I heard someone coming, I'm guessing you, and I bugged out."

"You didn't see anyone else?"

"If I had, he wouldn't be walking around," Kenny said with sudden intensity.

After Kenny left, Deputy Todd Orter brought in the next interviewee, that big guy who'd been shot in Glens Falls, Antonio Smith.

Before Alan could say anything, Smith said, "We should do this in private."

Alan hesitated.

"It's important," Smith said.

Alan nodded. He glanced at the deputy, who picked up on the hint just as fast as Alfred had earlier.

"So, Mr. Smith?" Alan said to Smith, once they were alone.

"Name's not Antonio Smith," Smith said, "although you should keep calling me that."

He produced a badge.

"I'm with the NYPD organized crime unit. Working undercover, obviously." He smiled ruefully. "You ask me, Grisham himself is no great loss, but it really fucks up our operation."

"You were after Grisham?" Alan said. He couldn't keep a touch of skepticism out of his voice. "The guy had his faults, but he was strictly local, and not involved with anything criminal, as far as I know. Other than his son, that is."

"The man was branching out, looking to upgrade out of Podunkville, whatever," Smith said. "We had information that Grisham was hooking up with some people of interest. Hoped we could turn him and get a line on them."

"Seems like kind of a long shot," Alan said.

"Absolutely, but our targets are a tough case to crack. Been trying to think outside the box on this one."

"What was Grisham involved with, anyway?" Alan said.

Smith shook his head. "Still confidential. It's mine to pursue. Without any interference."

For a moment Alan thought about telling Smith he was being pretty high-handed, for an officer out of his jurisdiction, but decided it wouldn't much impress the guy.

"Yeah, well," Alan said instead. "Whatever I can do to help."

"I'll let you know. For now, just keep this conversation between us."

"You're NYPD?" Alan asked. "Maybe you knew Jeff Sandil?"

Smith thought for a moment. "No. Don't think we ever met."

"Well, he's working for the Sheriff's Department here now. He was shot tonight."

"Serious?"

"He might be dead. I need to check in with the hospital."

Smith nodded. "It's a dangerous business, law enforcement."

Alan noted Smith's cold demeanor, but tried to tell himself that everybody deals with tragedy differently.

Smith stood. "Keep me up to date on your investigation," he said, and left without another word.

Alan stifled his irritation at Smith's peremptory command. You lose if you let someone like that get under your skin. That was just the way some of these big-city types were. Not all, by any means, but some, in Alan's experience.

The irritation came back stronger a moment later, though, when Alan realized that there had been no opportunity to ask Smith if he had heard or seen anything suspicious around the time of Grisham's murder, or if he could point to any likely suspects.

Not to mention, he hadn't gotten Smith's real name, either.

Alan put that thought on hold. He'd have to catch up with Smith later.

Still, Alan walked to the window looking out over the cars parked on Grisham's front lawn. In half a minute, he saw Smith get into his car. Alan made a mental note of the license plate number, as if he might run a check on it.

He wasn't sure why. Maybe just force of habit.

Elsewhere in the Grisham mansion, Charlie sat in front of the central control console for Grisham's electronic "smart house" system. The house might be more than a century old, but Carl had obviously installed some upgrades.

The computer controlled a variety of household functions, the heating and air-conditioning, lights, security alarms...and the intercom system.

Charlie carefully wiped his fingerprints from the control console, removing the evidence of how he had accessed the intercom connection to the library.

So, Smith was a cop, was he?

To date, Charlie's investigation of Smith had him pegged as some sort of organized crime middle management. If he was really a cop, that would take some heavy-duty, industrial-strength digging to confirm.

On one level, it wasn't really Charlie's business anymore. His agreement with Grisham was null and void, what with the big wiener in the process of taking the ol' dirt nap.

On the other hand, since when had Charlie ever let "none of his business" stop him before?

Besides, all information conceivably related to the investigation of Grisham's death was now of intense interest.

Yes, on that level, Charlie decided that "Antonio Smith" was very much his business.

Alan sat down in the chrome and steel chair in Grisham's library. Somewhere on the periphery of his thoughts he noted that the chair was astonishingly comfortable, for a pile of hard metal, but he didn't allow this to interfere with his primary focus.

Interviews with the various and sundry party guests hadn't produced much of anything he didn't already know. Alan closed his eyes, and allowed his brain to wander through the facts he'd learned so far.

The library door opened, interrupting his thoughts.

"Al?" said Deputy Orter. He entered the room with a middle-aged woman – short brown hair starting to gray, maybe 55, but solid and athletic looking.

"This is Mrs. Karen Carstairs," Orter said. "One of Jeff's neighbors. She's got something I thought you should hear directly from her."

"Mrs. Carstairs," Alan said, rising and shaking her hand. "I heard you were the one who found Jeff. I want to thank you for being there for him."

The woman shook her head. "Wasn't much I could do, I'm afraid. Guess it's a good thing he had someone there in his last moments, though."

Alan frowned. "He's not dead yet."

"Maybe not, but a head wound like that, there's really not much hope, is there?"

Alan glanced away quickly, then back at the woman, who suddenly looked embarrassed.

"I'm sorry, Mr. McMendell. He's a friend of yours, and here I am talking like this."

"It's okay," Alan said automatically.

"No," she said. "People say I can be too blunt. I was an Army nurse in Iraq. Dealing with what was left after improvised explosive devices didn't do much for my disposition."

"You're a veteran." Alan said. "Another thing to thank you for."

"Nice of you to say," Mrs. Carstairs said.

She put a hand on Alan's arm. "Your friend, Jeff. He said something before he, um, passed out."

Alan tensed, but willed himself to remain patient.

"It took Jeff a lot of effort to get it out, so I assume it must be important."

Alan felt his patience waning. Did anybody really call this woman blunt?

"What Jeff said was, 'He's good with information.' "

Alan took a step back. "Good with.... *Are you sure?*"

"That's an exact quote. I wrote it down right after the ambulance crew arrived," Mrs. Carstairs said. She handed Alan a sheet of paper obviously torn out of a small notebook.

Alan read the quote. He sat down and closed his eyes.

Lots of people were good with information, no doubt, but Alan knew only one person who made that claim on a regular basis.

"That's all he said, nothing more," Mrs. Carstairs added. "There is one other thing, though."

"Go on," Alan said, his eyes still closed.

"There was a strange car in the neighborhood. Older model, late '60s or early '70s. One of those muscle cars, with a turbo-whatsis sticking up out of the hood."

Alan's eyes opened.

"Its color?" he said. He knew the answer, but asked anyway.

"Black," she said. "But not shiny."

"Like a flat primer coat?"

"Yes, exactly."

For whatever reason, Alan hadn't interviewed Charlie yet. That was about to change, and then some.

"Deputy Orter," Alan said formally. "Find Charlie Payson. He's here in the house somewhere. Bring him to me."

Chapter 15.

Charlie gleaned all the information he needed from Deputy Todd Orter's cold attitude – something was about to hit the fan, and good ol' Charlie Payson stood squarely in the spray zone.

Well, this was not entirely unexpected, of course. Charlie walked quickly ahead of Orter, almost leaving the deputy behind. Best to meet Alan and find out how bad this was, and get it over with.

As he entered the library he caught sight of Alan, seated in Grisham's designer chair, of all places, eyes closed.

Bad indeed, Charlie thought. He hadn't seen Al looking this somber since the big guy's grandmother died years earlier. Or since Brian's funeral.

Charlie didn't like the way Alan was doing the eyes-closed thing, either.

It meant Alan was *thinking*.

"How's Jeff Sandil?" Charlie said, taking the initiative.

Alan's eyes opened. "Wondering if the charge will be murder, or just attempted murder?" he said.

Crap! Charlie thought. *Very, very bad indeed.*

"What?" Charlie said. "I'm a suspect because I'm showing some concern?"

"Let's skip the preliminary sparring," Alan said, standing and facing Charlie. "You're under arrest for the attempted murder of Deputy Jeff Sandil. Consider yourself Mirandized."

Charlie smiled and nodded. "Given all the evidence you must have, it's about time you arrested me."

"Is that a confession?"

Charlie's grin broadened. "Of course not. Don't be dense. I'm just saying it's about time you stopped being sentimental and acted on the evidence."

Alan shook his head. "Charlie, what the hell makes you

think I could ever be sentimental about you?"

"No, really, I'm proud of you, man," Charlie said. He held his arms out in the classic put-the-cuffs-on-me position. "You're finally starting to act like a real police detective."

He laughed and added, "Of course, you'll find out eventually that all that evidence you have against me is just the *tiniest* bit misleading."

Alan's face darkened. "You think this is funny?"

He grabbed Charlie by the scruff of the neck and slammed him against the wall, face first. He put all his weight into pinning Charlie to the oak paneling.

"I swear to God, Charlie, if you really shot Jeff, I don't give a crap what the damn grand jury says. You're history, you hear me?"

Other than a sharp cry of pain when he hit the wall, Charlie remained maddeningly calm.

"It won't come to that, I'm sure," he said, all too reasonably.

"It better not," Alan growled.

He took out his cuffs, and snapped them on Charlie's wrists.

"You know," Charlie said, "it occurs to me that we've been down this road before. You don't really think it's going to turn out any differently this time, do you?"

"That remains to be seen," Alan said. "By the way, you said, 'All that evidence.' How the hell would you know what evidence I have against you?"

"I don't. It's just logical. You wouldn't be arresting me if you didn't have evidence."

"Well, let's see," Alan said. "It occurs to me that I have witnesses placing you in the vicinity of three shootings in the last few days, including Jeff's. That's way too coincidental for anybody."

"Ah, coincidences. The epitome of circumstantial evidence," Charlie said. "You know, coincidences actually happen all the time. Mostly, we don't notice because they're usually not about anything important."

"Yeah, right," Alan said. He began walking Charlie to the

door. "How's this for a coincidence – we have Jeff's last words, that the person who attacked him was 'good with information.' "

Charlie raised an eyebrow. "*Really?* That's very interesting."

"What it is, is a perfect description of *you.*"

"I don't know about *perfect,* but I guess a reasonable person could say it does resemble me," Charlie said.

"So, if you didn't shoot Jeff, what were you doing out at his place?" Alan asked.

He waited for a response, but Charlie proceeded to clam up.

Getting in practice for the grand jury, Alan thought grimly. He didn't like that idea at all.

The thoughtful expression on Charlie's face didn't do Alan's peace of mind any good either.

Alan decided to attack the problem from different angle. "What about Grisham? Right now, you're looking pretty good for his murder."

"Based on what evidence?" Charlie said, breaking his silence. "C'mon, man. You don't really think I'd be dumb enough to kill Grisham with you less than a hundred yards away?"

"You forget how long I've known you. For a guy with your brain, you've done some pretty stupid things in your day."

"In my younger days, when my brain was still developing," Charlie conceded. "But here and now, what's my motive?"

"Other than the obvious, long-standing grudge between the two of you?" Alan said. "You can be arrogant enough to think you're doing the world a favor by offing Grisham. And arrogant enough to think you can get away with it, even with me just outside."

"Seriously, man. Why would I kill Grisham?" Charlie said. "I mean, he was a horse's ass. In an ideal world, that might be a capital offense, but I'm not going to make it one here in the real world."

"You and Grisham had some kind of deal going," Alan said, shifting his angle of attack again. "People kill for money."

This brought a smile to Charlie's face. "Actually, the vast majority of people *don't* kill for money. In fact, most people don't kill *anybody,* period. The percentage who do is really quite miniscule."

Alan grimaced.

"By the way," Charlie added, before Alan could say anything. "Speaking of coincidences, you do realize that your Mr. Smith was present for at least two shootings, even if he was on the receiving end at one?"

"He's not my Mr. Smith, and what's your point?"

Charlie clammed up again. He didn't say so, but it occurred to him that Henry was also somewhere nearby for two of the shootings.

At home that evening, Alan said to Alice, "You'll be happy about this part. I arrested Charlie Payson."

"About time," Alice said.

But she kept looking at him, and gently took Alan's hands in hers.

"What?" Alan said.

"It was hard for you, wasn't it?"

Alan smiled ruefully. "I've had better days."

"Do you think he really did it?"

"Hell, I don't know. I don't want to, but that's where the evidence is pointing. You know me and evidence."

Chapter 16.

Kenny waited in his car in the parking lot outside the County Sheriff's Department and County Jail.

One of his father's handguns, a Colt .357 magnum revolver Kenny had managed to hide from the police, weighed heavily in his jacket pocket.

Kenny's extensive experience on the receiving end of law enforcement led him to believe that Charlie Payson would be getting out on bail this morning.

McMendell had arrested Payson for the murder of Kenny's father.

A murder that Kenny knew had to be avenged.

Sure enough, Payson walked out onto the sidewalk around 11 a.m. Kenny didn't even think about pulling out the revolver. He just watched Payson stand there until a cab picked him up. Then Kenny started his car and followed.

Kenny's urge for revenge was strong, but his extensive experience on the receiving end of law enforcement had also led him to believe that being arrested didn't necessarily mean you were guilty.

True, to be honest, in Kenny's experience McMendell had never made that mistake. Nevertheless, the detective was still a human being, therefore theoretically capable of error.

Kenny had to be sure Charlie really was the one who killed his father.

Kenny recalled that McMendell once told him he had the instincts of a weasel, and the head of House Grisham was trying to be less weasely these days. Revenge had to be against the right person, or else what was the point?

Besides, weasely instincts or not, not shooting someone in

the Sheriff's Department parking lot was just freakin' common sense.

Alan spotted Smith across the restaurant. The big undercover cop was chowing down on a steak and fries lunch, while appearing to watch the parasailing out on the southern basin of Lake George.

"You're a hard man to find, 'Mr. Smith,' " Alan said, when he reached the table.

Smith looked up with clear annoyance. "Not hard enough. How'd you find me?"

"I'm not totally incompetent at my job."

Smith eyed Alan speculatively. "Hmm. Maybe not."

"I need to ask you some questions about the night Grisham was killed," Alan said.

"Thought you already made an arrest," Smith said.

"Only for the Jeff Sandil shooting, so far. I'm still working on the Grisham case. Both cases, actually. There's a lot of loose ends I need to follow up."

"And I got my own work to do," Smith said. "I don't have time for this, McMendell."

Alan considered this for a second, and said, "Yeah, that's why you're sitting here in this restaurant eating lunch. C'mon, man. You're a witness. You have to make time. Where were you when Grisham was killed?"

Smith stood up and faced Alan. Smith was only a fraction of an inch taller than Alan, but his attitude tried to exploit the difference as if it were a foot.

"I don't like being treated like a suspect."

"Then don't act like one," Alan said, ignoring the fractional height difference. "You're a police officer. You should know that's a standard question for a witness. So, what part of the house were you in?"

Smith abruptly chuckled. "Okay, so you can be feisty. All

right, all right. You got a job to do. Sorry to be so touchy. I was in the kitchen trying to find Henry Crane."

"Henry? What's your connection with him?"

"Got shot in his place, remember? I wanted to ask *him* some questions."

"Can Henry confirm that?"

"Doubtful. Said I was *trying* to find the guy. Never did. Not then, not the rest of the evening, now that I think about it. Don't know if he knows anything, but finding out more information is always a good idea."

"I want to interview Crane myself, but nobody's seen him," Alan said. "So, you were in the kitchen. Then what?"

"I heard gunshots. Two groups, three each, I think. There was a pause, and then another, different sounding shot. Then a lot of confused people running around."

"Anything else? Maybe something actually useful?"

"That guy you arrested. Payson? Saw him going upstairs shortly before the gunfire."

"Yeah, I already knew that. I saw him heading up there myself."

"There you go then," Smith said. "You don't need me after all."

Alan sighed. He suspected that, for better or worse, Smith was probably right.

Chapter 17.

Alan shook his head when he got the news.

"Charlie put up $250,000 of *his own money* to get out on bail? Huh. I guess I should've been a computer consultant."

Charlie settled into the office chair in front of his backup array of computers, profoundly glad that he was obsessed, for lack of a better word, about security.

The police had confiscated the computers in his Lake George office, naturally, so his file purge following Sandil's electronic incursion turned out to be a really good idea.

There was still plenty of data from Charlie's legit business to keep the cops busy – a ton of it in files right there on the main directory for any idiot to see, and another ton behind the standard passwords, firewalls, and encryptions one would expect from a computer consultant.

Nothing remained that was in any way incriminating, though.

Speaking of incrimination, Charlie was still seriously annoyed at having to put up $250,000 of his own money to bail himself out of jail. A damned nuisance, but he needed to be out.

Charlie liked to think that he could handle anything, but he was forced to admit that jail seriously did not agree with him. Way too confining. Especially now, when he had major work to do.

Charlie logged in on the central laptop. His backup array was similar to the one in police custody – a batch of overclocked laptops running Charlie's own heavily modified version of UNIX, with his own customized router and software linking them into a single, very powerful entity. The whole being more than the sum of its parts, as the saying goes.

This array was hidden on property Charlie owned, although not under his own name.

An hour later, Charlie was becoming increasingly frustrated.

He wanted to find out just how big a threat Antonio Smith was, and hopefully find something to use against the supposed undercover cop. Alan might be the one doing all the arresting, but Charlie's gut told him that Smith was at least as big a threat.

All Charlie had managed to pry out of the NYPD computers was that Smith was an upper mid-level wiseguy in Big Apple organized crime – exactly what you'd expect them to say for an officer on a deep undercover assignment.

Charlie noticed, however, that the records were missing key information, like exactly what the heck Smith did for the organization.

More troubling, Charlie was unable to find anything about Smith being an undercover cop.

It had to be in their databanks somewhere, no doubt buried quite deep, but "buried quite deep" never stopped Charlie before.

Then again, Jeff Sandil had found his way into the heart of Charlie's system, a location that Charlie had always considered impenetrable.

This fact forced him to contemplate the possibility that the NYPD was getting better at the forensic computer analysis game.

He didn't even want to think about the implications if that were true.

He finally gave up on the NYPD computers and logged off in disgust.

"I *am* good with information," he told himself. "If it's not in their computers, I'll find it someplace else."

Kenny fidgeted, shifting his butt on the seat of his car and repeatedly checking his father's revolver.

Impatience and the growing need to pee conspired to urge him to break into the house he had trailed Payson to, and confront the son of a bitch.

Yet he remained outside the house all afternoon, just watching the house and waiting.

In his criminal career, Kenny had met some pretty scary guys, and managed to keep it together. Payson, though, had probably killed his father, in a very bloody fashion. Not to mention, there was just something about the dude.

Kenny kept waiting....And, wondering just what the hell he'd really do in the confrontation. Did he really want this, he asked himself, or was this what he thought his father would want him to do?

You're the head of House Grisham, he told himself. *You decide, not him.*

Kenny was just beginning to tell himself that maybe the smart thing to do would be to call off this craziness, when the front door of the house finally opened.

Payson stepped outside and began walking to the garage a short distance from the house. He had a leather case, just the right size for a laptop computer, slung over his shoulder.

Before he could stop to think about it, Kenny was out of his car, revolver in hand behind his back, and approaching Payson.

He still wondered what he would actually do when push came to shove. He began bringing the revolver into play anyway when he had closed the distance between them to a few feet.

Kenny could've sworn that Payson was unaware of him,

but the dude suddenly exploded into motion.

Kenny was only beginning to duck when he felt the leather case, no doubt containing a laptop computer, smack the left side of his head.

The next thing the head of House Grisham knew, he lay flat on the ground with Charlie Payson standing over him. Payson held Kenny's .357 mag revolver in a two-handed grip.

"What's the matter with you? You back on crack or something?" Charlie said.

Kenny groaned. "You gonna make a clean sweep of it? Kill my father and me?"

"What the hell are you talking about?" Charlie said.

"McMendell arrested you for killing my Dad."

Charlie actually laughed. "Al arrests me all the time. It doesn't mean anything." He smiled sardonically. "He's arrested you a lot, too. You must know what that's like."

Kenny sat up. His head was clearing rapidly. He decided Charlie must not have hit him all that hard, which, all things considered, he found a bit surprising.

"In my experience," Kenny said, "to be honest about it, McMendell's only arrested me for things I've actually done."

"In my experience," Charlie countered, "it's been just the opposite."

Kenny pondered this for a minute, and finally decided exactly what he should do.

"Okay, so maybe there's some 'reasonable doubt' about you killing my father," he said. "I'm willing to wait for more evidence."

"Smart move," Payson said. "Responsible, even."

"Yeah, I'm all about responsibility these days," Kenny said. "Speaking of which, as head of House Grisham, I want some information from you."

Charlie raised an eyebrow. "*House Grisham?*"

"I know my father had you investigating Mr. Smith,"

Kenny said.

"So?"

Kenny's eyes shifted nervously. "So, as a show of good faith, you could give me whatever you dug up."

Charlie's face remained impassive. "Sorry, kid. My deal was with your father."

Kenny got to his feet and squared his shoulders. "I'm his heir. Whatever anybody owed him, they owe me now."

Charlie shook his head. "I'd be careful with that kind of talk. Look at it the other way. You're saying that whatever your father owed anybody, *you* now owe."

Kenny's voice rose in exasperation. "I *know* that. Why the hell do you think I need more information on Smith?"

The corners of Charlie's mouth twitched up briefly. "Logically put, but my services are not an inheritable asset. The answer's still no."

"You want me to look at things another way? Let's try this," Kenny said. "You know my father had information, about, uh, certain activities of yours. *That's* part of my inheritance."

Charlie laughed again. "Nice try, Kenny. Your father couldn't scare me with that crap, and neither can you."

Charlie started walking toward the garage again, then stopped. "A little advice, kid," he said over his shoulder. "Just because you look like your father, that doesn't mean you have to *be* like him."

"I expect a lot of people will be telling me that," Kenny said.

Charlie looked back at him. "I guess you do have a brain. For all your father's faults, maybe that's one good thing you got from him."

Almost against his will, Kenny said, "Thanks."

Charlie started walking, but Kenny said, "Um, my revolver?"

"I'll put it in a safe place," Charlie said.

"One other thing," Kenny said. His voice dropped sheepishly. "Can I use your bathroom, dude? I seriously need to pee."

Charlie chuckled. "Yeah, I guess you must have been waiting out here a long time. You can take a leak around behind the garage. The neighbors can't see you from there. Trust me, I checked it out."

After Kenny disappeared around the corner of the garage, Charlie opened the garage door and got into the Cooper Mini he'd stashed there.

Of all the times to get careless, he berated himself. What the hell was he doing not noticing that an amateur like Kenny was following him?

If the kid hadn't been sitting in plain sight out on the street, Charlie might actually have been taken by surprise.

That could've been irksome, especially when Charlie had far bigger issues to deal with, like what he needed to do about Alan.

Not to mention that other muscle-bound hulk, Smith.

Charlie now knew enough about Smith to label him the biggest threat to Charlie's future well-being.

Also not to mention, Grisham's information on Charlie was now in Kenny's hands.

Charlie didn't waste any concern about Kenny, as such. He worried instead about the fact that the mostly anonymous Charlie Payson and his unknown activities now seemed to be coming up on more and more people's radar.

And as if all that wasn't enough, Charlie knew he really needed to find Henry for a serious talk.

The guy was nowhere to be found at Grisham's after the murder. Charlie suspected the café owner and sometimes caterer witnessed something he shouldn't have, and was now hiding out. It would be – useful – to know what Henry had seen.

Calculating his priorities of the moment, Charlie decided Mr. Smith and Alan could wait, for a while. He'd let his subconscious work on those particular problems, while he occupied his conscious mind by tracking down Henry.

It sounded like a plan, anyway. Charlie expected that Henry might be the easiest problem to deal with, and he knew from experience that his subconscious frequently did a lot of good work when left to its own devices.

Charlie drove the Cooper Mini out onto the street, and began mentally assembling a list of places where Henry might hole up.

The Narrows of Lake George

Chapter 18.

The next afternoon, towering cumulus clouds rife with thunderstorm potential stood out starkly white against a deep blue sky over Lake George.

Alan, focused on his hunt, paid them little attention.

Heading south from Shepard Park in the Village of Lake George, Alan spotted Henry's speedboat just starting to pull away from one of the commercial piers between the park and Beach Road. Just when Alan had finally tracked down the surprisingly elusive cafe owner.

"Hey!" Alan yelled, and started sprinting for the pier.

Henry was already gunning the engine and either didn't hear or pretended not to. He motored off a little faster than the lake's 5 mph speed limit this close to shore, but not outrageously so.

Alan scanned the public village piers off Beach Road,

hoping to spot a patrol boat from the Sheriff's Department, or maybe the Lake George Park Commission.

No such luck.

Good God Almighty, Alan thought, spotting instead Charlie Payson's distinctive Maine lobster boat a couple piers over from the one Henry had used.

Charlie was on board, starting to cast off.

When Alan shouted this time, Charlie looked up and actually waved.

"I can't believe I'm going to say this," Alan said, hopping on board, "but follow that boat."

"Ah, so you want to talk to Henry, too," Charlie said.

Alan almost did a double take, but caught himself and said, "You got it."

"Cool," Charlie said. A deep rumble came from the stern as he fired up the lobster boat's 350-cubic-inch V-8.

Alan looked out on the lake and saw Henry departing the 5 mph shoreline zone, turning north and picking up speed.

Charlie cracked open his throttle, heading out at a sedate 5 mph.

"What the heck are you doing?" Alan said.

Charlie raised an eyebrow. "Are you saying I'm authorized to exceed the speed limit? I mean, I wouldn't want to break any laws or anything."

"Just hit it, smartass," Alan said, stifling the urge to throw Charlie overboard.

Charlie held off until they cleared the docks, then shoved the throttle forward. The sudden acceleration staggered Alan, but he managed to keep his balance.

By the time they left the 5 mph zone, they were already exceeding the 45 mph speed limit for the open lake.

"How fast can this thing really go? It's no Donzi," Alan shouted over the roar from the engine.

Charlie shrugged. "You've seen my car, right? You think I

haven't souped up my boat?"

Charlie looked thoughtful for a moment. "On the other hand, I've also helped Henry with some engine work on his boat. If he doesn't want to talk to us, there might not be a damn thing we can do about it."

"Just great," Alan said.

"By the way," Charlie added. "Isn't this a conflict of interest for you, or something? Consorting with a suspect?"

Alan had been debating in his own mind whether he had just done something damned crazy by getting on a boat with the prime suspect in the shooting of his partner.

On the other hand, it might be an opportunity to apply more pressure.

Instead of responding to Charlie's question, Alan said, "Hell of a coincidence, you and Henry both deciding to go boating at the same time."

"Like I said, I want to talk to him, too. He's been surprisingly difficult to track down." Charlie glanced at Alan. "Besides, I've told you my position on coincidences."

"By the way," Alan said. "We found gunshot residue on the clothes you were wearing at Grisham's. That puts you at the shooting."

"Yeah, but what shooting?" Charlie countered. "I was target shooting out at the Dunham's Bay rifle range that afternoon. That's where the GSR came from."

Alan allowed skepticism to creep into his voice. "Sounds like another coincidence. Anybody see you there?"

"Maybe. I'd have to ask around."

"Don't bother. That's my job," Alan said.

Charlie gave a "whatever" shrug. "Suit yourself," he said.

Alan began to feel the steady roar of the engine penetrating his bones as they kept up the chase, racing over the water at full throttle.

"You should get a better muffler for this thing," he

hollered.

Charlie said nothing, while concentrating on a slight course change to get a better intercept angle on the wake of another speedboat.

The lobster boat sliced through it with ease, kicking up spray that glinted brightly in the afternoon sunshine.

Alan didn't say so to Charlie, but the boat's performance impressed him. Here they were, flying along probably somewhere north of 50 mph, and the ride was surprisingly smooth.

He also had to admit to himself that he was impressed by Charlie's seamanship. Alan hadn't even seen the wake until they were in it. For being a lifelong resident of the area, he'd actually spent very little time boating on Lake George. He told himself, as he had often told himself before, that he should get out on the lake more often.

Charlie motioned towards Henry's boat, about 600 yards ahead of them.

"I hate to say this, but Henry doesn't seem to be paying any more attention to the speed limit than we are. We're maxed out, and he's pulling away," Charlie said.

"Not by much," Alan said. "Stay with him. Are you sure this thing can't go any faster?"

"She's maxed, and maxed is maxed, man. Like you said, she's no Donzi." Charlie shook his head. "I knew I was going to regret not getting around to installing a nitrous oxide system. That'd give us another 50 horsepower, easy."

Alan flipped open his cell phone, but couldn't hear anything over the engine and was forced to text.

"No good," he said to Charlie, a minute later. "The Sheriff's Department boat is down for maintenance, and the Park Commission and EnCon boats are back in the village at Million Dollar Beach. We're on our own."

"Great," Charlie said. "Henry's got a good half mile on us."

"Maybe we'll get lucky, and he'll stop in Bolton."

"Never rely on luck," Charlie said. "Casinos make lots and lots of money off people who do."

"You could be right," Alan said, as Henry kept on going straight up the lake, leaving them farther and farther behind.

"He's practically a mile ahead," Charlie said when Henry reached The Narrows, where Tongue Mountain shoves in from the west, constricting the lake from more than two miles wide down to less than one.

Henry disappeared into the jumble of state-owned islands that fills The Narrows.

When the lobster boat reached the islands a little over a minute later, Charlie eased off on the throttle. The V-8 roar dropped to a more tolerable rumble as they slowed to a relatively sedate 15 mph.

"We can't go tear-assing through here," Charlie said. "There's too much boating traffic from all the state campsites on the islands."

Alan looked unhappy, but said nothing.

"This might not be that bad," Charlie said. "Henry must have slowed down, too. We probably gained some ground on him. Or water, I guess I should say."

After 10 minutes of nosing around the islands turned up no sign of the elusive cafe owner, he began to look less confident.

"It looks like maybe Henry's outfoxed us," Charlie said. "Man, who knew the guy had it in him?"

"Keep looking," Alan said.

"Aye aye, cap'n," Charlie said.

A blustery gust of wind drew Charlie's attention to the west.

"Crap," he said, pointing to the ridge line of Tongue Mountain looming over the lake. "I was afraid those cumulus clouds were developing awfully fast. We're in for it now."

Alan looked up to see an immensely tall, dark mass of cloud lumbering over the ridge. Heavy sheets of rain whipped down from it.

As if on cue, a bolt of lightning ripped out of the thunderhead with a sharp electric *crack,* striking a tree on an island 100 yards to port. A booming rumble of echoing thunder drowned out the boat's engine noise as easily as if it never existed.

"I think you might be right," Alan said.

Charlie guided the boat into the lee of the next island, where they found one of the piers installed for island campers and picnickers.

Charlie killed the engine and tied the boat off just as the downpour began pounding on the lobster boat's cockpit roof and windshield, hitting with a sound like handfuls of gravel.

The sky darkened until it might as well have been nighttime. Alan felt the temperature drop a good 20 degrees.

Another bolt of lightning *cracked* into the island just east of them.

Alan looked at Charlie. "Now what?"

Charlie looked out at the thunderstorm and grinned. "Enjoy the show! What else?"

For the next 20 minutes, the two of them hunkered down in the boat's cockpit, saying nothing, watching the storm rage around them.

Microburst winds howled through the trees, snapping off the occasional branch. Sheets of rain, sometimes laced with pea-sized hail, hit the boat so hard that Alan was sure the windshield was going to implode.

Lightning struck all around them, lighting the gloom with brilliant flashes. Thunder rolled almost continuously.

Eventually, the rain slackened as the thunderstorm rumbled on up over Shelving Rock Mountain to the southeast.

Tongue Mountain after a storm, from Bolton Landing.

Charlie stepped out of the cockpit as the sun reappeared. "Man, that was a good one!"

"Not that good," Alan said. "Take a look at the front of your boat."

Charlie turned and saw what appeared to be a maple tree now growing out of the deck at the bow. A three-inch diameter branch, snapped out of a tree by the wind, had landed vertically and punched through the decking.

"Son of a bitch," Charlie said. He practically dove into the crawl space under the deck.

A minute later, he called out to Alan, "No significant internal damage, at least that I can see so far. Gimme a hand. I'll push up from below while you pull from above."

As Alan made his way forward, Charlie added, "Watch your step. I don't need a big hulk like you crashing through the deck and landing on my head."

"Very funny," Alan muttered. Getting a good look at the branch, he added, "It's lucky for us this sucker didn't land a

135

few feet farther back."

They made quick work of removing the branch and carrying it onto the shore.

Charlie pronounced the damage to the deck "basically cosmetic," but taking another look below, he sounded less optimistic.

"Hard to say whether there are any structural issues," he said. "We're in no danger of sinking, but I'd prefer to avoid high speeds until I can do a more rigorous analysis. To be on the safe side."

He looked over at Alan. "You still want to do the Captain Ahab thing and keep tracking down Henry?"

"Let's head up to the north end of The Narrows, in case he holed up like we did, but my gut says he's long gone," Alan said.

His gut appeared to be right.

"Pack it in," Alan said 20 minutes later, when no sign of Henry could be found.

Charlie headed south at a leisurely pace through the islands, and accelerated to a moderate cruising speed of around 25 once they left The Narrows.

"Hey, Charlie," Alan said, as they passed by Dome Island. "Do you remember that summer after we graduated from high school that you, Brian, and I camped out on Dome Island here? We had a hell of a thunderstorm that night, too."

"Alan...." Charlie said.

"I know, I know. You don't want to talk about what happened to Brian. Does that mean I can't reminisce about the good times?"

"I guess not," Charlie said. "The guy was something else, wasn't he?"

"Yeah. We almost got arrested for trespassing, but Brian spun that outrageous tall tale and talked the boat patrol officer out of it."

"Good thing for you," Charlie said. "An arrest record might have put a crimp in your law enforcement career."

"That would have been a hard way to find out that Dome Island is an off-limits nature preserve," Alan said, although he didn't really think a trespassing infraction would've made that much of a crimp.

They lapsed into silence until they reach the Lake George village docks.

"Well, this was a big waste of time," Alan said.

"Look on the bright side," Charlie said, tying up the boat. "Being out in a boat on Lake George is never a waste of time, bitchin' thunderstorms and all."

Alan scowled at him. "For a guy facing a charge of attempted murder of a police officer, you're awfully upbeat."

"That'll blow over," Charlie said.

"Only if you can prove you're innocent," Alan said.

Charlie shrugged. "See you in court. If it gets that far."

Alan shook his head. "Overconfidence. You don't have many weaknesses, but that's always been one of them."

Chapter 19.

Smith's cell phone rang at 9 o'clock that evening. He didn't recognize the cell phone number on the caller ID, but decided to answer anyway.

"Hi, 'Antonio,' " said the voice on the other end. "We, as they say, need to talk."

"About what?" Smith said.

"Our mutual acquaintance, Jeff Sandil."

Smith said nothing.

"Antonio?" the voice said.

Smith finally answered. *"Charlie Payson.* What would you know about Jeff Sandil?"

"Everything." Charlie paused a couple seconds himself, then said, "I'm...good with information that way. But then, you know how that goes. You figured out who I am quickly enough."

"A simple deduction," Smith said.

"Tonight, at the Grisham casino, 11 o'clock," Charlie said.

"The Grisham what?"

"Ha! That's a good one," Charlie said, and hung up.

Smith closed his cell phone, and put it back in his pocket. He mentally kicked himself for not making the effort to learn more about Payson right after the bastard was arrested. Now, he had very little time to try to give himself an edge before the confrontation.

After a minute's thought, he pulled his phone out again. *There's all kinds of edges,* he told himself, and punched in the number for that big local cop, Alan McMendell.

"McMendell, this is Antonio Smith," he said when the guy answered. "Just got a call from that suspect of yours, Payson. Wants to meet me to talk about Jeff Sandil. I smell a setup. You want in on it?"

"Charlie called *you* about Jeff?"

"My gut says he's going to play some kind of con. Try to pin the blame on someone else," Smith said.

"And he called you?"

"What, after you arrested him, you think he's going to call *you?*" Smith said. "Look, Payson and Carl Grisham had some kind of deal going. You know that, right? I'm starting to think Payson was the hump who shot me. He shot your partner, and if you ask me, he killed Grisham, too. The guy's fucking dangerous. I want backup when I meet him."

McMendell said, "Just tell me one thing. What the hell was Grisham into?"

Smith sighed. "Yeah, whatever, if that's what it takes to get you off your ass. Illegal gambling. Grisham had an underground casino in Lake George. We play our cards right, I figure we can nail Payson for being part of that, too."

"All right then," McMendell said. "When and where?"

Smith gave him an address in the Village of Lake George. "Tonight. Payson expects me at 11. We'll meet outside at 10:45," he said, and hung up.

Alan closed his cell phone. It occurred to him to wonder what, if anything, "Antonio Smith" was up to.

Charlie, of course, was definitely up to something. Of that, Alan had no doubt. Again, the question was, what?

Plus, this bit about Grisham and gambling he had just managed to pry out of Smith. That made all kinds of sense, the more Alan thought about it.

But Charlie and illegal gambling? Could he really be a

party to that? Then again, it might help explain how Charlie happened to have a quarter million bucks lying around to put up for bail.

Alan's cell phone rang again. He checked the caller ID. Speak of the devil.

He answered. "Charlie. What now? You ready to confess?"

"Droll, as always," Charlie said. "Actually, I have some information you'll be interested in."

"Information. Something you're so 'good' with."

"Damn straight," Charlie said, apparently ignoring the reference. "Do you want to hear this or not?"

"I don't know. Do I?"

"Jeez, don't overwhelm me with enthusiasm."

"You gonna tell me or not?" Alan said.

"There, you see? I knew you'd be interested," Charlie said. "You've been trying to track down some illegal gambling in Lake George, right?"

Alan decided not to be surprised that Charlie knew about that investigation.

"Yeah. And?" Alan said.

"And, I can lead you right to the underground casino."

Charlie gave him an address in the Village of Lake George. The same address Smith had given.

"Tonight. Eleven o'clock," Charlie said.

"So, why are you telling me all this?" Alan asked.

"Call it a gesture of good faith."

"Some might call it an attempted bribe," Alan said.

"I'm always being misjudged. I try to help out law enforcement, and this is the thanks I get?" Charlie said, and hung up.

Interesting, Alan thought. Charlie wanted him and Smith together, at what might, or might not, be an illegal gambling casino.

Alan decided he wouldn't miss this for the world.

Canada Street, the main drag in the Village of Lake George, at night

Chapter 20.

At 9:20 p.m., Charlie stepped outside the entrance to Grisham's casino into an alley on one of the back streets in the Village of Lake George.

The casino had been as quiet as a grave when he arrived 20 minutes earlier and made his phone calls to Alan and Smith. Charlie figured that with Grisham murdered, the rest of the casino personnel must have decided to lie low for a while.

He had suspected that would be the case, and was gratified to be right. The last thing he needed was pit boss Frank Banfield and company getting in the way.

Charlie tensed when he heard footsteps coming down the alley. He expected Alan and Smith to come earlier than 11, of course, but not this early.

Charlie knew that Al would suspect he was up to

something. Odds were that Smith would suspect likewise.

Squinting in the dim light leaking over from the well-lit Canada Street business district, Charlie made out a figure coming around the corner.

He saw a man, carrying a heavy backpack, medium height, portly....Son of a bitch.

The man was Henry Crane. Henry froze when Charlie stepped out to meet him.

"Henry," Charlie whispered. "What the hell, man. I've been looking for you everywhere."

"You shouldn't be here," Henry said, his eyes shifting nervously from side to side. "I've started something, and if I don't finish it I think I'm going to go crazy. It's better for you if you don't get involved."

"I'm pretty sure I'm already involved," Charlie said. "C'mon, I'm your friend. Talk to me."

Henry's shoulders sagged. "Maybe you're right," he said. "Not being able to tell anybody must be half of what's driving me crazy."

Henry looked down at the ground, refusing to meet Charlie's eyes.

"I murdered Carl Grisham," Henry said.

"You?" Charlie said, raising an eyebrow. "Let me guess. You stabbed him with a knife?"

"Yes," Henry said, still avoiding Charlie's eyes. "Right in the heart." He glanced up briefly. "What, you don't think I'm capable?"

"You might be capable, if you knew where the heart was," Charlie said.

Henry's forehead wrinkled. "Whattaya mean?"

"I mean, you didn't stab Grisham in the heart. The knife wound wasn't fatal."

"But... all that blood? I thought for sure I must've killed him."

"You would have, eventually, without emergency medical treatment anyway. What really killed the guy was a bullet in the brain."

"But... but... I didn't shoot him. I don't even own a gun."

"Well, somebody else did. *You* didn't kill Grisham," Charlie said.

"You're sure?" Henry said, finally looking up.

Charlie thought he saw a look of hope in Henry's eyes.

"Absolutely, my friend," Charlie said. "In spite of your best efforts, you're not a murderer."

Charlie watched Henry trying to digest this fact. He thought he saw the exact instant when it truly sunk in.

Henry bent over, as if he were going to throw up.

"Thank God," he said simply.

Charlie grinned. Henry had his problems, including an obsessive personality and an unexpected reckless streak. The guy would bear watching, but it looked like the he still had the right reaction to being a killer.

Charlie wondered when he himself had lost that.

"What's in the backpack?" Charlie said.

Henry looked up at him, a bit sheepishly. "Dynamite. I was going to blow up the casino."

"A noble thought," Charlie said. "Why don't you let me worry about that?"

"But, man, the way they treated me...."

"Let it go, Henry. Trust me. You'll feel better."

Charlie eased the bag off Henry's shoulder and set it on the ground.

"See? You feel lighter already."

Henry grinned in spite of himself. "You know, I think I actually do."

Charlie hefted the backpack, estimating the weight at about 50 pounds.

Henry damned well ought to feel lighter, he thought.

Charlie looked inside and found numerous sticks of dynamite, blasting caps, remote detonators, and various other demolition-related odds and ends.

"Jumping hell, man. Where'd you get all this stuff?"

"My sister's husband owns a demolition business up in Silver Bay," Henry said. "I worked for him summers when I was in college."

Charlie's brain connected a few facts. "Just north of The Narrows. That's where you went on your boat this afternoon," he said.

Henry nodded. "I recognized your boat following me. Sorry I didn't stop, but...."

"But, you didn't want to talk to me," Charlie said.

Henry nodded again, still a little sheepishly.

Charlie hefted the backpack again. "Does your sister's husband know this stuff is missing?" he asked.

"Uh, well, no."

"That's okay," Charlie said. "We can worry about that later. Right now, I'll take care of it."

"Are you sure? Maybe I should just take it back."

"Hey, if you can't trust me with 50 pounds of dynamite, who can you trust?"

"I'm not sure I like the sound of that," Henry said, but he smiled when he said it.

"Don't worry," Charlie said. "I'll put it to good use. Right now, you should get your ass out of here."

Henry turned, then said over his shoulder, "The kid, Jason. He won't get hurt, right?"

Charlie put a hand on Henry's shoulder. "I believe there is hope for you. The place is deserted, so I don't think that'll be a problem."

"Charlie, I don't know what to say."

"I'm not asking you to say anything. Just get out of here before McMendell and Smith show up. And whatever you do, don't ever even imply anything about this to anyone, especially the cops."

Henry shook Charlie's hand. "You're a good friend, Charlie."

"That's what I keep trying to tell people. Now scram."

Henry grinned and took off.

Charlie observed the new spring in Henry's step. A burden had definitely been taken off the man's shoulders. Not that he didn't have a potential assault-with-a-deadly-weapon charge hanging over him, but still.

Charlie slung Henry's backpack over his shoulder.

Funny, he thought, *it doesn't seem all that burdensome to me. Now, just what could a friendly fellow like me find to do with approximately 50 pounds of high explosives?*

He glanced at his watch, and wondered exactly how much time he had before Alan and Smith showed up.

Charlie had enough time, he calculated, to make a few modifications to his preparations.

Like his old Marine drill instructor had drilled into him, "Think ahead. Preparation is always one of the keys to success."

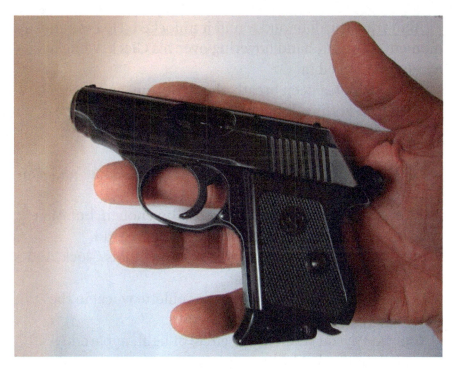

Small .22 semi-automatic

Chapter 21.

Alan found Smith waiting in the alley outside the casino at 10:30 p.m.

"You're early," Alan said.

"You too," Smith said. "Payson'll expect us this early. Wouldn't want to disappoint him."

As they approached the door, Smith said, "This stinks of a trap, right? You know this guy. He likely to just start shooting when we come in?"

"Not a chance," Alan said. "Even if he planned to shoot us eventually, he'd want to talk first. See what we know."

"Your call," Smith said. Drawing a SIG Sauer 9-millimeter automatic, he waved Alan ahead. "You first."

Alan tried the door and found it unlocked. He hesitated a moment, his right hand hovering over his Glock, while his adrenaline kicked in.

Then he took a deep breath, drew the gun, and entered.

He found nothing but a few feet of hallway leading to a descending flight of stairs, dimly lit by a light from the basement.

Alan heard Smith rack the slide on the SIG Sauer and step in through the door behind him.

Alan glanced back. Smith looked calm enough, but Alan caught him wiping beads of sweat off his forehead.

Alan smiled grimly, readjusted his grip on his Glock, and slowly descended the staircase.

A single lamp hanging above the roulette wheel in the middle of the room cast harsh shadows.

Charlie Payson stood in the circle of light, apparently unarmed, but he held what appeared to be some sort of remote control.

What looked like an excessively large pile of dynamite sat on the roulette wheel's betting table. A red light flashed steadily on and off from a piece of electronic hardware on top of the pile.

"Gentlemen," Charlie said. "You're right on time."

Smith growled and aimed his SIG Sauer at Charlie.

"Easy there, Antonio," Charlie said, gesturing at the dynamite. "I'm holding a dead man switch. If my thumb lifts off the button, *kaboom!*"

"See, McMendell?" Smith muttered. "*Told* you the guy's fucking dangerous."

"You have no idea," Charlie said.

Alan snorted. "Gimme a break, Charlie. You're bluffing. Whatever else you might be, you're not suicidal."

"If one of you shoots me, that's kind of a moot point," Charlie said.

Alan nodded reluctantly. "Yeah, right. Smith, we better take him at his word. For now."

"Don't like this at all," Smith said, but he lowered his gun.

"Excellent," Charlie said. "Now we can talk like reasonable people."

He waved the remote in Smith's direction. "I finally got the lowdown on Smith just this evening. This yahoo's been saying he's an undercover cop. That's a load of bull. He's actually a part-time leg breaker for the mob in the Big Apple."

Smith smirked. "What'd I tell you, McMendell? He's trying to pull a scam, pin the blame on somebody else. That leg breaker crap is my cover story. He's been taken in by it."

"You didn't let me finish," Charlie said. "I said you're a *part-time* leg breaker. Your full-time organized crime job is finding out stuff – digging up dirt that can be used against people, cracking computer systems, learning who's got how much money hidden where – in short, *information.*"

Charlie turned to Alan. "As in, '*He's good with information.*'"

Smith glanced at Alan. "What the hell does that mean?"

"It means the son of a bitch is making a good try, I'll give him that," Alan said.

"Al, c'mon, have I ever lied to you?" Charlie said.

Alan snorted.

Charlie persisted. "Seriously, man. Sure, I deceive you, but I always do it by what I *don't* tell you. I never lie to you outright."

"So, if Smith's the murderer, what's his motive?" Alan said.

"McMendell? What is this crap?" Smith said.

"Simple," Charlie said, ignoring Smith's irate interruption. "Our Mr. Smith blames Grisham for the attempt on his life. Jeff Sandil was NYPD. He knows too much about Smith."

Smith shook his head, and aimed his SIG Sauer at Charlie again. "Enough bullshit. I'm ending this."

"It's not bullshit, man," Charlie said, taking a step back.

Alan abruptly pivoted to point his Glock at Smith.

"I know," Alan said.

Smith reacted instantly, grabbing Alan's right wrist with one hand and firing a shot in Charlie's general direction with the other, and following up with a kick at Alan's groin.

Alan twisted, and the kick glanced off his hip.

Smith tried to turn his pistol on Alan, but Charlie appeared next to them and wrenched the pistol away.

Smith, still holding Alan's wrist with one hand, used his free hand to swat Charlie in the head.

Charlie went down. The SIG Sauer went flying.

Alan used the opportunity to knee Smith in the gut, producing a grunt but no other noticeable effect.

Alan took body blows and a punch to the nose from Smith's free hand until he rammed Smith against a wall and kneed him in the gut a couple more times.

Throwing all his weight into pinning Smith against the wall, Alan panted out, "What was the idea, Smith? Make it look like the cop and the murder suspect killed each other in a shootout, leaving you in the clear?"

"Something like that," Smith grunted.

Smith shifted position slightly, then pushed off the wall and tripped Alan, sending them both crashing to the floor.

Alan twisted so that Smith didn't land on top of him, but the impact knocked Alan's Glock out of his hand.

Smith followed up with another punch to Alan's head.

Momentarily half dazed, Alan instinctively reverted to his college wrestling days, using his legs to control Smith's lower body, and catching Smith's left arm in an arm bar.

Smith struggled wildly, trying to use his massive strength

to break free.

He threw more punches with his right arm, but didn't have the angle to put any real power into them.

Alan held on grimly, feeling the blood leak out of his nose, absorbing the hits, calling on every ounce of his own strength to maintain the ragged edge of his control.

Some small stray part of Alan's mind noted, with great satisfaction, that Charlie really had been bluffing about the dead man switch.

"Give it up, Smith," Alan said, when he still held control after what felt like an eternity.

"Advantage does seem to be yours," Smith gasped. He slowly began releasing the tension in his body. His free arm dropped to his side.

The earsplitting gunshot from behind took Alan completely by surprise.

As did the 9-millimeter hole that appeared in Smith's forehead, slamming Smith's head to the floor.

"What the hell?" Alan said. He jumped up and furiously slapped Smith's SIG Sauer out of Charlie's hands. "I had him. You didn't have to do that."

"Didn't I?" Charlie said. He nodded at Smith's body. "Check out his right hand."

Alan's expression remained furious, but he stepped around to Smith's right side anyway.

From there, he could clearly see the small, .22 semi-auto still in Smith's hand.

"You didn't see him pull that out of his pocket, did you?" Charlie said. "He was about to put several holes in your chest. I expect you would've found that inconvenient."

Alan glared at him, saying nothing.

Charlie went on, "I'm betting ballistics will match that gun to the other shootings."

Alan thought about it for a moment.

Then he said dryly, "Nice shot."

Charlie said, "I believe the protocol in this situation requires me to respond, 'But I was aiming at his chest.' " He shrugged. "Poetic justice, though, isn't it?"

Alan rolled his eyes.

"Well, this is convenient," said a new voice.

Alan and Charlie looked up to see Frank Banfield and Jason at the foot of the stairs.

Banfield was carrying an honest-to-God Thompson submachine gun, as if he were a 1920s gangster.

"Crap and a half," Charlie muttered.

"I had a gut feeling something was going on here tonight," Banfield mused, as if talking to himself. "Now I find Smith, McMendell, and whoever this other guy is. Sad to say, they fought and they all ended up killing each other."

The pit boss grinned as he carefully aimed the Tommy gun. "That leaves this territory open for *me* to run a casino."

Chapter 22.

"Boss, come on," Jason said, tugging at Banfield's sleeve. "I didn't sign on to committing murder."

"Don't wimp out," Banfield growled. "This job ain't all fun and games. You gotta learn the hard parts too. Now stop distracting me."

Alan and Charlie glanced at each other, wordlessly agreeing on a plan of action. Alan would dive for Smith's .22, while Charlie dove for the pistol Al had slapped out of his hand.

And, then they'd hope for the best, like maybe if they were really lucky Banfield would only be able to nail one of them before one of them got him.

Banfield resettled the Tommy gun on his shoulder.

Before Alan and Charlie could move, another figure, medium height and portly, appeared on the stairs behind Jason.

The figure shoved the kid out of the way, grabbed Banfield by the shoulder, spun him around, and drove a fist into the pit boss's face.

Banfield dropped flat on the floor, unconscious, nose broken.

Henry Crane stood over him, breathing hard, clutching his fist with his other hand.

"I owed him one," Henry said. He sagged into a nearby chair. "Dammit, I think I might have broken my hand, though."

"What the hell are you doing here?" Charlie said. "I mean, thanks, man. But...."

"After thinking about it, I decided to hang around outside.

Back you up, you know?" Henry said. "When I saw Frank and Jason show up, I figured they probably weren't part of your plan."

Alan looked over from one of the casino tables, where he had found a paper napkin he was using to stop up his bloody nose.

"This was a plan?" he said.

"I was going to induce a confession out of Smith to murdering Grisham and shooting Jeff Sandil," Charlie said. "I'm guessing that maybe you had the same idea, but it didn't exactly work out that way."

He shrugged. "Close enough for government work, though."

Alan put handcuffs on Banfield, who was starting to wake up.

Then Alan looked around. "Hey, where's that kid?"

"Jason?" Charlie said. "He ran up the stairs just after Henry decked our erstwhile pit boss, here. Chances are he's long gone by now. He's a small fish anyway."

"Very small," Henry agreed.

Charlie nodded at Henry. "How's the hand?"

Henry held up his damaged hand and gingerly flexed the fingers.

"I guess it's not really broken," he said. "Hurts like hell, though. There's a kitchen in back. I think I can find some ice in the freezer."

"Get some for my nose while you're at it," Alan said. Turning to Charlie, he said, "Help me get this character, what's his name?"

"Frank Banfield," Charlie said.

"Yeah, whatever. Help me put him in my car."

"You're going to leave him in your old Taurus?" Charlie said.

"No, I've got an unmarked police car tonight," Alan said.

"We can lock him in there for now."

After stowing Banfield in the car, Alan and Charlie headed back towards the casino.

"So, let me guess. You found out the truth about Smith by hacking the NYPD computers?" Alan said.

"Of course not," Charlie said. "I called NYPD headquarters and asked. God knows I love computers, but if I limited myself to them, I wouldn't get half the intelligence I come up with."

"The NYPD just handed this over to *you,* of all people, over the phone?"

Charlie grinned. "They, uh, seemed to have the idea that they were talking to you. I think their caller ID might even have said the call was coming from the Sheriff Department offices."

"Hrrmm," Alan commented.

"Besides, you can be very persuasive," Charlie continued. "It's almost like The Force having a powerful influence over the weak-minded. Not to mention, information that someone's *not* an undercover cop doesn't seem to be all that top secret."

Alan glowered at Charlie, but instead of tearing Charlie a new one about impersonating a police officer, he said, "You could've told me what the deal was with Smith."

"Would you have believed me? Let me set up a sting on him?"

"Maybe...."

"Yeah, that's what I thought," Charlie said. "It was my neck on the line, man."

Charlie added, "So, how did *you* know Smith was a phony?"

"Same as you, sort of. Something about the guy just wasn't right. I finally got around to calling the NYPD after you set up this meeting, although my approach involved *unofficial* channels. I have some old friends in the NYPD."

"You're good with information, too, is what you're saying," Charlie said.

Alan nodded. "I am a trained detective, after all."

They were at the entrance to the alley when Henry came running full tilt out the casino door.

"*Fire in the hole!*" he yelled. He threw a bag of ice to Alan, said, "Sorry, I just couldn't resist," and kept running.

"*Frak!*" Charlie said, diving to the ground. "*Hit the deck!*"

Alan stared at him for a second, then remembered the big pile of dynamite on the roulette wheel. He dropped to the ground and put his hands over his ears.

The **KABOOM!** came just a few seconds later.

Alan felt the shock wave flatten his clothes against his body. Bits of concrete cinderblock and other debris rained down around them. Inevitably, several car alarms began honking and warbling from neighboring streets.

Charlie sat up and surveyed the heavily-damaged building and shook his head.

"Man, I don't envy you, having to take this mess to the grand jury," he said.

Alan stood up and grunted. "Not to mention, deciding what to do about you."

"Moi?" Charlie said, putting his most innocent expression on his face.

"Knock it off. This is serious," Alan said. "I owe you for saving my life...."

"Three times, actually. Two and a half, at least," Charlie pointed out.

"....but I have a duty to put you in jail, and probably throw away the key. Henry, too, when I catch up with him."

Charlie sighed. "Yeah, the old moral dilemma thing. Welcome to *my* world."

"*You* have moral dilemmas?" Alan said.

"Jeez, man, I would've thought that was obvious."

"*Jeez, man*," Alan fired back. He suddenly broke out laughing, maybe a little too hard. "Charlie Payson has morals. Who knew?"

Charlie rolled his eyes. "I'm so glad I could cheer you up, but I thought you wanted to take this seriously."

Alan got a grip on himself and stopped laughing. "Yeah, I guess I do. So, what do you expect me to do in this impossible situation you've put me in?"

"What you think is right. I mean, I really didn't save your life so you'd owe me one."

"And, what is right?"

"I can't answer that for you," Charlie said. "You have to make your own decision."

"Swell," Alan said.

He thought for a minute, then flipped open his cell phone and began making calls.

Chapter 23.

Alan and Sheriff Tellerman met Jeff Sandil's neurological specialist, a Dr. Maggie Nelson at the Albany Medical Center, after receiving the welcome news that the deputy had finally regained consciousness.

"Sometimes," Dr. Nelson told them, "a .22 round can ricochet around inside the skull, causing all sorts of damage. With Officer Sandil, as near as we can tell the bullet traveled straight back, more-or-less between the two brain lobes."

Alan noticed the sheriff watching the doctor intently.

Dr. Nelson went on, "The bullet then lodged in the bone at the back of the skull instead of ricocheting."

The doctor led them down the hall toward Jeff's room. "It caused damage, of course. Lacerations from bone fragments where the bullet entered, and some trauma along the bullet pathway.

"All told, though," the doctor added, "it could have been a hell of a lot worse."

"He'll be okay, then?" the sheriff asked.

Dr. Nelson smiled ruefully. "That remains to be seen. To paraphrase Yogi Berra, we won't know until we know. Until yesterday we kept him in a coma with his body temperature artificially low. That minimizes neurological damage from swelling in brain and spine trauma cases, and, like I said, there was less damage than we expected."

Dr. Nelson put a hand on the sheriff's arm. "I don't want to give you false hope, though. This was a very serious head injury. Memory problems and other cognitive challenges are likely. Returning to police work? I'd be surprised."

"Can we see him?" Alan asked.

"I think he'd like that," Dr. Nelson said.

A week later, Charlie almost literally bumped into Alan outside the courtroom at the County Municipal Center.

"I hear Jeff Sandil's doing better," Charlie said. "That's good."

"Yeah," Alan said. "He's got a long road ahead of him, but at least you can see the guy, the personality, still there."

Charlie looked down at his artificial left foot. "I know something about long roads. I can talk to him, if you think it would help."

"Answer me one question, and I'll think about it."

Charlie raised an eyebrow.

"When Smith and I were fighting, why didn't you just leave? You could have even blown the place up with Smith and me, and you'd be totally in the clear. Instead, you hang around and save my life."

"Not totally in the clear," Charlie said. "Charges against me would still be pending with the grand jury." He grinned. "Of course, you know me and grand juries."

Charlie checked his watch. "Speaking of the grand jury, I don't want to be late."

He turned and headed toward the courtroom.

Alan called after him. "What about my question?"

Charlie paused and said over his shoulder, "I'd miss you arresting me all the time, what the hell do you think?"

Three days later, Charlie stepped out of the courtroom and into the afternoon sunshine, free and in the clear.

He found Alan leaning against Charlie's old Chevy Nova.

"How's it going, Al?" Charlie said, taking the initiative. "Crime in the county under control?"

Alan snorted. "Well, you're still on the loose."

The Lake George Casino Gamble

Charlie grinned. "Yeah, that makes it Charlie Payson, two, grand jury, zero. And half a point for Henry Crane."

"Yeah, I hear he plea bargained down to a lengthy probation, and only has to do a couple months in minimum security," Alan said.

"By the way, thanks," Charlie added.

"For what?" Alan asked.

"For what you *didn't* tell the grand jury."

Alan shrugged. "The DA didn't ask."

Alan laid a heavy hand on Charlie's shoulder and added, "Things can't stay this way forever. You know that too, don't you?"

Charlie's grin faded. "If that means you're going to start talking about Brian, you already know my answer. Brian was a big boy. He knew the risks."

"I knew the risks, too. So why didn't you bring me along, too?"

"You didn't know the risks. You still don't."

"What the hell does that mean?"

Charlie didn't answer.

"Are you ever going to tell me what I want to know?" Alan said, pushing harder. "What I *need* to know?"

For a moment, Charlie appeared for all the world to actually give the idea serious consideration.

"There's a lot I'd like to tell you, man. Maybe even should tell you," he said.

Alan leaned forward, not even aware he was doing so.

Charlie saw the look in his eyes, and sighed. "But I can see that even that is saying too much. The bottom line is, I honestly think you're better off not knowing."

Charlie watched the hurricane-force storm grow in Alan's eyes, then fade to a mere thunderstorm.

"What a load of bull," Alan said.

Charlie shrugged.

Alan looked Charlie in the eyes for several seconds, then finally looked away.

A moment later Alan thumped his hand on the roof of Charlie's primer-black Nova.

"You ever gonna put a decent paint job on this thing?" he said.

Charlie nodded. "Someday, man. Maybe someday."

Chapter 24: Charlie's loose end.

"How's it going, Kenny?" Charlie said, barging unannounced into what was now Kenny Grisham's office in the Grisham mansion.

Kenny occupied the big leather chair behind what had been his father's desk.

"Whatta *you* want?" Kenny said. "And that's 'Mr. Grisham' to you. I'm beginning to think I don't like you anymore than my father did."

Charlie grinned. "I wouldn't have it any other way." He took a seat without being asked. "By the way, it's a shame about that casino of yours blowing up last month."

Kenny narrowed his eyes. "I don't know what you're talking about. I don't have any casino in Lake George."

Charlie snorted, and said in a passable Inspector Clouseau accent, "*Not anymore.*"

Kenny rolled his eyes and sighed. "Is there some reason for this visit, Mr. Payson?"

The humor left Charlie's eyes. "Kenny, I don't expect you to confess to shooting Antonio Smith at Henry C's Cafe."

Kenny winced noticeably, but said nothing.

"After all," Charlie continued, "I ended up doing what you tried to do."

"And you somehow managed to do it in legal self-defense, apparently," Kenny said. "How'd you pull that off?"

"Just helping out a friend," Charlie said. "Which is also why I'm here now."

A worried look suddenly grew on Kenny's face. He began reaching for the hefty can of pepper spray holstered underneath the desk. Kenny would have preferred a handgun, like his father, but there was no way Kenny could get a pistol permit, and he judged that possession of an illegal gun would be a bad idea in his present circumstances.

Charlie held up his hands. "Easy, Kenny. You won't need whatever's under that desk. I don't want to help out anyone 'in self-defense' again. At least for a while. The DA's suspicious enough of me already."

Kenny stopped reaching, but didn't relax. "So?"

"So, Smith is a moot point, but Jeff Sandil's another matter entirely," Charlie said. "You're going to confess to shooting him with a shotgun after that drug bust in Glens Falls."

"You're crazy," Kenny said, glaring defiantly. "The guy can't testify after what Smith did to him. Without Sandil, they've got no case against me."

Then the bluster drained out of the kid. He looked down at the desk. "Besides, I was stoned out of my mind on crack that night."

He raised his head and looked Charlie in the eyes. "I don't get that way anymore."

"You shot a *cop*, not some guy the world's better off without," Charlie said. "There has to be some consequence for that."

Kenny leaned forward, still looking Charlie squarely in the eyes.

"Listen, Charlie. I know it probably freaks you out that I look just like my father when he was my age. It freaks me out a little too, but *I'm not him*. I'm *trying, dude*."

Kenny slumped back in the chair. "Besides, my father's dead. I'd call that a hell of a consequence."

Charlie stared back into Kenny's eyes for several long seconds. "Huh. Okay. Maybe." After another pause, he added, "When I accused you of shooting Smith, you didn't deny it."

"Jeez, dude, I'm sorry about Sandil, but the world *is* better off without *Smith*," Kenny said. "I thought we were on the same page there."

"You're not trying to tell me you attempted to kill him to make the world a better place?"

"No," Kenny admitted. "Smith was messing with my family. I wanted to put a stop to it."

"That attitude, at least, is understandable," Charlie said, "but that still leaves us with Jeff Sandil."

Kenny closed his eyes for a second, and took a deep breath. "If the DA indicts me about Sandil, I'll plead no contest," he said.

Charlie raised an eyebrow. "You'll also drop your father's police brutality suit against Alan McMendell?"

"Already did that," Kenny said. "The criminal complaint, too."

"Really? Maybe you *are* trying." Charlie smiled ruefully and shook his head. "Man, I came in here prepared to be a real hard ass and nail you to the wall. Then you had to go and make my life more friggin' complicated by trying to reform yourself."

Kenny ventured a smile. "I could try to be more like my father, if that would help."

"Very funny," Charlie said. He stood. "Well, I think my work here, as they say, is done. For now. I'll be in touch."

"Wait a minute," Kenny said. "You said you were here to help a friend. McMendell, right? Is he okay with this?"

"This conversation is just between you and me," Charlie said. "I have no control over Alan. I assume he'll go with the evidence, as always, and push to the full extent of the law. You're right, though. Not having Sandil testify drastically weakens their case."

Charlie put his artificial left foot up on the chair, made a minor adjustment, then looked up at Kenny again.

"Anyway," Charlie said, "whatever all that leads to, you'll have to live with it."

"I guess so," Kenny said. He shifted uncomfortably in his chair. "This trying-to-reform-yourself stuff isn't easy, is it?"

Ain't that the truth, Charlie thought, on his way out the door.

The amphitheater in Shepard Park, Village of Lake George

The Lake George Casino Tip
A very short prequel to The Lake George Casino Gamble

by David Cederstrom

Alan McMendell lost sight of his target in the swirling mass of tourists thronging Canada Street in the Village of Lake George.

He picked up his pace, using his imposing six-foot, two-inch height and heavily muscled shoulders to work his way through the crowd.

The midafternoon summer sunshine beat down out of a cloudless sky, making Alan regret having left his sunglasses in his old Ford Taurus. Clouds had masked the sun when he left the car, but the clouds were gone now. That was North Country weather for you. Another half-hour, Alan figured, and they could just as easily be in the middle of a thunderstorm.

For now though, Alan squinted his restless brown eyes against the sun. He finally picked up his quarry again – a slender, red-haired young man named Donny, entering Shepard Park across the street.

By the time a large enough gap opened in the traffic for Alan to jog across the street, Donny had disappeared into the park.

Alan had no trouble reacquiring his target, though. Donny stood on the stage of the park's open-air amphitheater. He was talking to some more-or-less teenager, a tourist by the look of him.

Donny pulled a small plastic bag out of a pocket. The teenager began reaching for his wallet.

Alan cursed. He'd warned Donny about this, how many times was it now? It was time to let actions speak louder than words.

Alan moved swiftly and silently down the amphitheater steps, coming up behind his target and the teenage would-be drug buyer.

"Hello, Donny," Alan said. Softly, but with a certain edge in his voice.

Donny jerked around, eyes wide in a half-panic, and then he saw Alan.

"Jeez, McMendell, don't scare me like that, man," Donny said.

"Scare you?" Alan said. "What do you have to be scared about? Or should I say, who?"

Alan glared at the teenager Donny was about to sell to, and pulled out his County Sheriff's Department Investigator badge.

The teen opened his mouth as if to start some smart remark, but quickly thought better of it.

"Later, dudes," he said, trying to be cool, but moving off at about twice as fast as a truly nonchalant pace.

Alan shook his head. "Donny, we've talked about this. You're not supposed to be selling. In broad freakin' daylight, no less."

"Man, c'mon," Donny said. "How'm I supposed to get information to snitch to you if I don't act the part?"

"Whether I buy that argument depends on what you have to snitch," Alan said.

"Right down to business, as usual," Donny said.

He gave Alan an address in Glens Falls. "Cocaine, man. They got a half a pound or so they're baggin' up for street sale."

"Yeah, we already know about them," Alan said, stifling a yawn. "What else?"

Donny grinned. "Well, didja know Kenny Grisham's involved with 'em?"

Alan forgot to act bored. "Really?" he said.

Kenny had been a thorn in Alan's side for years, even if only for minor offenses. Alan had arrested Kenny several times, but there'd been no convictions, thanks to the high-powered lawyers hired by Kenny's high-powered banker father, Carl Grisham. An opportunity to nail Kenny once and for all was valuable information indeed.

Donny nodded. "I knew that'd get your attention, man." He shook his head. "I hear the wacko kid's carryin' heavy firepower, too. A double-barrel, 12-gauge, sawed-off shotgun, if ya can believe that. Loaded with solid-slug deer hunting loads."

Alan pressed a little skepticism into his voice. "You sure about that?"

"As sure as I ever am about anything," Donny said.

Alan conceded the point. "Okay, you've earned your keep. I'll let your other activities slide. This time."

"You're a stand-up guy, McMendell," Donny said, accepting the $50 bill Alan held out.

Donny turned to leave, but he was apparently feeling magnanimous. He added, "There is one other thing. It's outside my pharmacological area of expertise, ya understand, but I hear there's an underground gambling casino somewhere here in the village. Poker, blackjack, maybe even a roulette wheel. The state still hasn't approved casino gambling in Lake George, right?"

"Yeah," Alan said. "The legislature's working on that, but

it's still a felony."

"I'll see if I can find out anything else," Donny said. "I'm kinda curious about this one myself."

He turned to leave again.

"Donny?" Alan said, allowing that certain edge to creep back into his voice. He held out a hand.

Donny didn't even pretend to not know what Alan was driving at. "Oh, man," Donny griped, but he handed over the plastic bag.

Alan kept his hand out.

"Jeez, McMendell, for a stand-up guy, you can be a real hardass sometimes." Donny reached into a pocket and produced two more bags and put them in Alan's hand.

"Good stuff?" Alan asked.

Donny sighed forlornly. "Primo weed, man."

Alan stuffed the bags into a pocket for later disposal, as he watched Donny take his time ambling back to Canada Street.

A casino in Lake George? Alan thought it seemed pretty unlikely. Then again, maybe that reaction was what an illegal casino operator would count on.

Once the upcoming raid on the cocaine dealers in Glens Falls was over, Alan decided, he'd take a look into this casino rumor.

Excerpt from

The Bacchus Effect
Book 1 in the Lake George Mystery and Adventure series
by David Cederstrom

Available on Amazon

"You don't have to choose this path, Adam. You could..." Charlie Payson said.

"I could what? 'Turn away from the Dark Side?' As I believe the younger people say, get a life." Adam Hartwicke barked a sharp snort of laughter. His shotgun barrel dipped.

Charlie was growing really tired of options that included the possibility of getting shot, but this was the opportunity he'd been waiting for.

Just two steps.

That was all he needed. Then it'd be flesh and blood against flesh and blood, no weapons.

He wouldn't need any weapons to kill the old bastard.

It seemed to take forever to get there, but at a step and a half, Charlie began allowing himself some serious hope. He could see Hartwicke moving, but even slower than himself. The old man couldn't bring the gun up in time. No way in hell.

Charlie barely noticed the sound when Hartwicke fired, but the impact of buckshot ripping through Charlie's left foot stunned his entire system. Time slowed even further, to a near standstill.

Friggin' idiot! Charlie sneered inwardly. *Try and live with this choice. If you can.*

Excerpt from

Target: Lake George

Book 3 in the Lake George Mystery and Adventure series
by David Cederstrom

Due out on Amazon in 2024.

The foot hanging at an odd angle out of the New York State Police patrol car's door caught Charlie Payson's attention.

Charlie barely glimpsed the car in the Adirondack Northway median, as he sped by in the Interstate's northbound lane between Exits 20 and 21, on his way to Lake George in northern New York.

The guy's probably just taking a nap, Charlie tried to tell himself.

And, if there was trouble, didn't cops always consider the person who finds the body the prime suspect? He didn't know that for sure. He'd only heard it on some TV cop show, but he thought it sounded like the way cops would think.

Charlie had grown tired of being a suspect. He was finally in the clear now, as well he should be, no matter whether district attorney Joe Hanrahan liked it or not. Charlie seriously wanted to keep it that way.

All this flashed through Charlie's brain in the fraction of a second before he stepped on his brakes.

"Fragging hell," he muttered. No doubt this would soon become one more good deed that would not go unpunished.

Charlie pulled onto the shoulder of the road. He slammed his custom '72 Chevy Nova SS muscle car into reverse, and backed up to where he had a good view of the State Police cruiser.

Yeah, nobody napped in a car with his foot at an unnatural angle like that.

The cruiser sat sensibly in the shade of a stand of pine trees, avoiding the heat of the mid-afternoon, late August sunshine, rear end toward the highway, driver's door open, with the foot jutting out awkwardly. Charlie noted that the foot showed no motion at all.

Charlie waited for several cars to pass – carrying plenty of potential witnesses for the prosecution, no doubt – then walked across the highway.

He approached the car, scanning the ground for footprints and tire tracks. The ones Charlie saw were vague and indistinct in the grassy median, but he avoided disturbing them anyway.

A crow stuck its head out of the car door.

It gave Charlie an ugly look, *cawed* harshly, then hopped out and flapped into the air.

It landed in a tree 20 yards away and *cawed* again.

"Same to you, buddy, " Charlie said.

He looked inside the car. The presence of the crow, and the coagulated state of all the blood, told him he was way too late to do any good. The wind shifted suddenly, wafting a confirming stench into his nostrils.

Charlie reflected that at least it was a good thing he had arrived before the crow got down to business.

He noticed that the body was in plainclothes, not the

uniform one would expect a state trooper on duty in a patrol car to be wearing.

How the hell do you get yourself into these things? a part of Charlie's mind asked, in a brief spasm of cold amusement.

Then he pulled out his cellphone and called his once and sometimes friend, County Sheriff's Department Investigator Alan McMendell.

Unseen and unheard, an MQ-9 Reaper military drone, A.K.A. Predator B, flew at 20,000 feet overhead. Its ultrahigh-resolution cameras recorded a vast swath of the territory below in exquisite detail.

If anyone had noticed the drone and inquired about it to the military, he would've been told it was simply on a training flight out of Hancock Air Base in Syracuse, about 110 miles to the west.

Excerpt from

Land of the Free

A spinoff from the Lake George Mystery and Adventure series
by David Cederstrom

Due out on Amazon in 2024.

Chapter 1: The Blues and the Greens

Normally I feel right at home in bars, but shadowing my target into the Droppe Out Tavern & Bistro gave me the impression I must have died and gone straight to hell. I'd never seen anything like it. We're talking an eclectic cross between an American Legion hall and a biker bar, with maybe a few ferns thrown in "for atmosphere."

That might sound harmless enough, especially on a chilly summer night on the Pacific coast in northern California. But so help me God, the bar's featured performer, wearing a blue tux and lit up in a spotlight on stage, billed himself as "Buck Waldowski, Master of the Electric Accordion."

If my target hadn't stepped into the joint, I could have gone the rest of my entire life without ever being subjected to this so-called "entertainer."

For that alone, the target *deserved* to die.

I discreetly checked the Para-Ordinance P12 compact .45 automatic in the shoulder holster under my old brown leather jacket. The time to make my move couldn't come soon enough.

Name? My friends call me Willy. Willy Cook. Some of you might have heard of me. My life isn't exactly a well-kept secret anymore, although I'd be better off if it were. I always found anonymity to be very useful in my line of work. Maintain a low profile, that was my credo.

Then a few tabloid articles here, a couple of *Insider* episodes there, and all of a sudden a guy can kiss his anonymity goodbye. Such fame is fleeting, of course, and maybe you're not into the "entertainment" media. I never know who might remember my youthful face, though. Maybe even my target, his dorky looks notwithstanding.

Oh yeah, one more thing. You can look it up in those tabloid articles anyway, so I might as well get this over with.

Willy is short for *Wilmer*.

Yeah, that's right. I've got the same name as the cheap gunsel in *The Maltese Falcon*. I don't know what my old man was thinking, but I had the last laugh, considering that I actually became a cheap gunsel.

Well, come to think of it, not so cheap. No, not so cheap at all.

Be that as it may, I was earning my fee that night, and then some. Buck Waldowski, self-proclaimed "Master" of the godforsaken electric accordion, was making my teeth grind like the gears of an old school bus driven by some middle-aged dude sporting a bad haircut.

My target, on the other hand, was downing brewskis at a table near the stage. Rapt attention lit his otherwise bland, dweebish face. He actually drummed the table with his hands, keeping time to the music, if that's what you want to call it.

The Buckster cranked up the volume on the amp and belted out noise that bore a suspicious resemblance to "Stairway to Heaven." I swore that if I *hadn't* died and gone to hell, I'd be up for committing suicide in no time.

I tell ya, the mook even tried to play *the Blues*. On a freakin' electronically amplified *accordion*, understand?

What a god-awful way to be spending my 30th birthday.

After what seemed like about a year and a half, Bucky finally took a break. I hoped it wouldn't take a year and a half to kill the memory of what he'd just done. I considered going backstage and breaking the Buckmeister's fingers, as a service to all humanity, but that's when my target headed for the men's room.

I stretched my arms, reconfirming the weight of the .45 hanging from my left shoulder. Finally, it was time to make my move.

Oh, just relax, wouldja? I wasn't going to do anything really *bad* to the guy. I'm a reformed individual these days, allegedly, courtesy of "the love of a good woman." I'd sacrificed a lot to gain the love and respect of a woman I *know* you've heard of. Trust me on this, even I'm not sure how I pulled off romancing a big-time movie actress like Melanie Astor, but I bet you remember what all those tabloid articles were about *now*.

Okay, so after taking care of business, maybe later I'd just go backstage and dance a polka on Waldowski's accordion, instead of his fingers.

I followed my target into the men's room. He stood six feet tall, almost even with me. Scrawny as a heroin-chic model. Hemp-fabric clothes. My age plus five. Pretty harmless looking, overall, especially considering that I out-muscled him by probably 40 pounds.

Still, he'd offended my wealthy industrialist client mightily. (I'd tell you my client's name, but there's that client-gunsel confidentiality thing.)

My client fingered the target as some sort of self-styled, New Age Green eco-warrior type. We hoped he'd lead us to an ultra-radical, enviro-terrorist bunch of hotheads who call themselves Earth Over All Else. I'm as environmental as the next guy, but the Over Alls are into *extreme* monkey wrenching, such as blowing up wealthy industrialists, if you catch my drift.

You remember, they're the ones who crashed a CBS Evening News broadcast last year. Faces concealed by green hoods, they warned environmental violators, "If you're going to call us eco-Nazis, by God we'll *be* eco-Nazis."

Three CEOs had died in Over All explosions since then. I'd picked up hints that my client topped the Over Alls' list, and that they were planning an incident that would dwarf their previous acts.

This understandably made my client nervous.

As I silently closed in on my target, however, he still didn't strike me as the terrorist type. On the other hand, I should know that looks can deceive.

I dropped a heavy hand on the target's shoulder.

He spun around instantly, in one smooth, flowing, eye-blink of motion. Raw intelligence flashed across the suddenly non-bland face.

I jumped back on reflex, as if I'd stepped on a rattlesnake. I'll bet even money on myself against anyone in hand-to-hand combat, but when a guy moves like that, I gotta pay attention.

It's the same way *I* move.

The dude started to go into a combat stance, then tried to cover up the move by stumbling.

"I, I'm sorry, you startled me," he stammered.

His face had gone all bland and dorky again, but I could see the way his eyes were sizing me up. Apparently what he saw convinced him he'd blown his cover.

Maybe the smirk on my face tipped him off.

He started to drop into a combat stance for real this time.

Before he could get set, I smacked him up-side the head. You can supply the fancy martial arts term, if you like. I'm content to say I smacked him. Hard, but not as hard as I can.

I'll be darned if the dude didn't shake it off.

"Are you sure you're old enough to be in a bar, kid?" he said.

Yeah, my youthful face is one of those that keeps on looking like I'm 19 or 20. Makes a lot of people underestimate me. Which is useful, except when it's blasted annoying, like always getting proofed.

I grinned.

"You tryin' to annoy me, Slim?" I said. "Take the easy way out. All I want is information."

For an answer, he took half a step back, feinted left, and came up with a weird, whip-fast move I'd never seen before.

I barely saw the foot he bounced off my temple.

I rolled with it, but not quite as fast as I should have. Hefty impact flashed through my head.

He hit hard, for such a scrawny dude. Not hard enough. My old man boxed professionally. People joked he could take a hit better than Rocky Balboa. I guess I inherited the Cook Family thick skull.

"That your best?" I said.

I danced back, taking a couple of deep breaths and wiping a trickle of blood away from my eye. Here I'd been talking about people underestimating *me*. I needed a moment to ratchet my mindset up to max. This was turning into a tougher job than I ever expected.

The dude attacked again.

A direct frontal assault this time. He subtly shifted at the last fraction of a second into a twisting grab at my wrist, which he used to throw me into the wall of a toilet stall.

With a wrenching screech, the sheet-metal wall half-collapsed, leaving me seriously off balance.

I saw him close in with another blindingly fast kick at my head.

I punched up at his heel.

That sent the foot skimming over my head, and the rest of the dude tipping over backwards.

I took a heavy shot in the shoulder from his second foot as he went down, I'll give the shifty S.O.B. credit for that. The dude paid for it, though, leaving an opening for me to slam a swift kick into his left hamstring.

I would have preferred to connect with his nuts, but hey, I'll take what I can get.

The dude rolled and sprang to his feet, limping slightly.

By the wild look in his eyes now, yeah, I believe he's the terrorist type.

I thought briefly about the .45 in my shoulder holster. I left it there. How often does a guy get to work out with somebody this good?

We circled each other warily. I forced him to circle right, so I could attack on his weak-leg side.

"You're good, Slim, but I'm just as quick and who knows how much stronger," I said. "Why don't you just tell me what I want to know, before somebody gets hurt?"

"Overconfidence, Cook," he said. "It'll be the death of you."

(See? I *told* you he might remember my face.)

I laughed.

"Man, first a good fight, now death threats," I said. "And here I thought this evening was going to be totally dismal when that Waldowski butcher started playing."

"Shut up!" The dude's face twisted. "Buck is a *genius!*"

He snarled like a Rottweiler and recklessly launched

himself at me again.

Call me shocked that anyone could defend Waldowski, let alone lose his cool about it. That didn't stop me from staying alert for any mistake the dude might make. Like losing his cool, for example.

I met his launch with a right cross. I really got my hips into it. Exactly the way my old man began teaching me as soon as I was old enough to put on a pair of boxing gloves.

The dude hit the floor.

I guarantee he didn't spring back to his feet this time.

"I could've warned you, being an accordion fan is hazardous to your health," I said.

He was too unconscious to appreciate my insight.

I searched him quickly. Five hundred and change in cash, and a driver's license that said his name was Arnold Hawking, exactly like it was supposed to. Nothing to indicate membership in a group as wacked-out as the Over Alls.

After half a minute he started coming around. Pretty fast recovery, considering the shot I gave him, but that was okay. How else could I ask the questions I needed to ask?

Hawking's eyes opened and swirled back into focus. Oh yeah, definitely the eyes of a fanatic.

"Betrayer of the Earth!" he said. "All betrayers must pay!"

Yeesh. A fanatic all right, complete with wacky slogans.

Well, what did I really expect? Hawking was probably the primo representative of the estimated half-dozen people who made up the Over All roster.

Even sprawled on a men's room floor, he seemed intent on keeping the "eco-Nazi" spirit alive.

"Earth First!, Greenpeace, the Earth Liberation Front, all those weak sisters draw the line at taking human life," Hawking said. "The Green fire in the *Earth Over All Else* heart will show them how to get *real* results. It's going to be big, Cook, bigger than anything anybody's ever done. Bigger than 911!"

His lips twisted back from his teeth. "Maybe Buck and I will let you appreciate it from ground zero."

The faint rustle of a tuxedo behind me gave me *almost* enough warning.

I turned just in time to see Waldowski swinging his accordion into my face.

Very hard.

One more reason to hate accordions. I had just enough time to be glad I'd at least been given the chance to damage the blasted thing after all, even if it had to be with my forehead.

Then lights flared brilliantly, followed by the usual swift fade to black.

Also by David Cederstrom, to be on Amazon eventually:

109 Absolutely Essential Rules for Avoiding Trouble: From the Inconsequential and Blindingly Obvious to the Subtle and Life-Altering

Some humorous rules, some serious rules, but all darn good advice, and/or a chance for Dave to go shooting his mouth off about various subjects.

How Johnny Won the War

An anthology of short stories, including contemporary adventure, mystery, science fiction, and even a little romance (almost).

The Adventures of Boowoo:

Tales of a Young Rescue Dog

By Buppa and Uncle Dave

A children's book written by Dave's father, Alan Cederstrom (Buppa) and Dave (Uncle Dave)

Boowoo, a happy-go-lucky young dog named for the way he barks, is rescued from the dog pound and has lighthearted adventures with his newfound family.

Also, now available on Amazon:

The Brimstone Hill Gang

By Harriet Riley Cederstrom

Harriet (Dave's Mom) writes with warmth, humor, and insight in 17 (mostly true) recollections of her life growing up in rural Maine in the 1930s and '40s.

David Cederstrom was born in Maine and has called the Lake
George-Queensbury-Glens Falls region of northern New York home
ever since his family moved there when he was three years old. He
earned a BA in anthropology from the State University of New York
and has worked as newspaper reporter and photographer for more
than 40 years.

Made in the USA
Las Vegas, NV
09 May 2024

89724050R00105